D0098835

THE
ICE TRAIL

THE
ICE TRAIL

Anne Eliot Crompton

Methuen, New York

Library of Congress Cataloging in Publication Data

Crompton, Anne Eliot.
The ice trail.

SUMMARY: Persistent memories of his earlier life
compel 15-year-old Tanial to flee from his Abenaki Indian
captors and journey during the winter from the northern
shores of Lake Champlain to the English settlements.
[1. Abenaki Indians—Fiction. 2. Indians of North
America—Captivities—Fiction] I. Title.
PZ7.C879Ic [Fic] 80-17062
ISBN 0-416-30691-8

Acknowledgement:
Indian songs used as chapter headings are from *The Path on the Rainbow*,
edited by George W. Cronyn, with permission of Liveright Publishing Corporation. Copyright 1918 by Boni & Liveright, Inc. Copyright 1934 by
Liveright Publishing Corporation. Copyright renewed 1960.

Manufactured in the United States of America
Designed by David Rogers

Published in the United States of America by
Methuen, Inc.
733 Third Avenue
New York, N.Y. 10017

Contents

THE
ICE TRAIL

1) The Flight Feather

The heart knoweth his own bitterness.
PROVERBS 14:10

Two near-grown boys crouched on a root that snaked above ice-filmed water. Like branches sprouting from the root, they leaned slightly apart, perfectly still.

Hopefully they watched the glow of the sunset fade from Lake Champlain. Twilight is the hour of the hunter, when day creatures seek their beds and night creatures rise and set out. But on this late autumn evening nothing moved near the screen of cattails. The pale cold sunset was empty.

The dark boy sighed and unstrung his bow.

Reaching to unstring his own bow, the blond boy paused. He was large and firmly built. Braids like bands of sunshine framed muscular shoulders. Under its soot coating his face was surprisingly pale. He was called Tanial Waligit, Handsome Daniel.

He had not always been called that. When the Abenaki Indians had first captured him five years ago, in 1703, they had called him "Tanial Awakon." One day Tanial had refused to answer to that name. He would not even look around when they called him "Awakon," for he had learned that awakon meant slave.

Defiance won him threats and blows. Tanial looked up stubbornly from one angry face to the next. He had to look up because he was young and small. Big Katetin loomed huge; dreamy old Mhlosses looked like a brown dead pine, bending to catch his hair with twig fingers. Then Tanial's friend Molsemis came and took his hand. And Molsemis' father Awasos placed a hand on each boy's shoulder.

Now, hesitating to unstring his bow, Tanial remembered Awasos' teaching. His blue eyes narrowed, his hands tightened on the bow. Then warning instinct became hearing. From behind and above came a whistling sound that strengthened very fast, swooping near.

Tanial drew the bow. The next instant a swan sailed over his head and dropped to the water. The bow twanged like a singing voice. Swan and arrow met above the water.

Tanial jumped down off the root. His feet and legs were bare—better cold feet than frozen wet deerskins! He waded out, grabbed the flopping bird, and wrung its neck.

Molsemis had not moved. Still and quiet, he crouched on the root, the unstrung bow useless in his hands. As Tanial splashed back to shore, Molsemis rose smoothly to his feet. The name "Molsemis" means "young wolf." Graceful as a wolf, Molsemis tied on his leggings and stepped into his moccasins. All the while, he looked sideways at Tanial and at the limp swan. Dressed, he faced Tanial with determined good cheer. "You win," he declared. "That is one fine bird."

Tanial agreed. "We will be glad for it if the hunters do not return."

"They will be back tonight. Mhlosses saw them. They have been drunk, he says, but now they are coming."

Tanial grunted. Old Mhlosses' dreams and visions so

often proved right that Tanial wondered if the magician, the powwow, might not be in league with the devil. Certainly the preacher back home would say so. Mhlosses' form of prayer was so different from the White, Yengi form, he could hardly be praying to the same god.

Molsemis turned and started up the low bank. Tanial laid the swan down and tied on his leggings. Scuffing into his moccasins, he looked out once more across Lake Champlain. He could hardly see the other darkening shore, but he looked toward the south as if to a holy place. With all his soul, he longed to rise like a swan and fly south over the endless forest.

Inspiration struck. Quickly Tanial snatched up his swan by the left wing. But that wing was twisted; at one time it had been broken. That must be why the swan had been late, flying south. It would be a bad omen.

Tanial stretched out the right wing. This wing was perfect. Wind and power still seemed to vibrate in its feathers. And the swan had been flying south, to the country of Tanial's dreams.

He pulled out a long white flight feather and dropped it into the pouch that dangled at his waist. Falling into darkness, the feather came to rest against a small, frozen, warped book. Feather and book nestled together in the bottom of the pouch, two pieces of a secret, magic puzzle.

Swan in hand, Tanial trotted up the bank after Molsemis. The quiver bobbed against his shoulder. His frozen legs warmed rapidly in the comforting deerskins. His heart warmed, too. Once more he had proved his worth.

Awasos will be pleased, he thought proudly, when he comes back with the hunters. A cold finger of worry touched Tanial's mind and hastily withdrew. Worry was a White, Yengi fault, for which Molsemis would tease him. The Abenaki world was far too dangerous for the luxury of worry. Better to meet danger and sorrow only when, and if, they came.

His strong trot now brought him in sight of the cluster of tents which to Molsemis meant home.

Dark among the pine trees, two bark wigwams stood together near a glowing fire pit. A third, smaller wigwam stood grumpily off by itself. This was Mhlosses' spirit tent. From it sounded a soft drum tap and the old man's quavering chant.

Like flitting shadows, camp dogs circled the fire pit. A small black dog broke away from the circling pack and bounded up to Tanial. Crouching and wagging, it pawed at his leggings. He kicked it aside—not too hard—and made for the fire.

A rich smell of corn wafted up from the pit. "That's the last of the cornmeal," he thought. He swung his swan for the women to see.

Big Katetin, Molsemis' mother, turned from her scraping frame. She had a deerskin stretched on the frame between two pines. Now that it was too dark to see, she came to the fire. Katetin was broad and strong, her back stooped by countless burdens. Her black eyes beamed welcome to Molsemis, suspicion at Tanial. Then, seeing the swan, she gave him a grudging smile.

After Katetin, old Talaz hopped birdlike to the fire, nodding kindly to both boys. Katetin called Talaz mother, but Tanial felt sure that she was not really Katetin's mother. Perhaps she was an older sister who had taken the mother's place as Tanial's own sister had done.

Quickly he brushed that thought aside. He tried never to think of home and family. Firmly he turned his attention to the French kettle sitting on the coals, half full of corn, acorn, and cattail mush.

Small brown hands held a bark bowl under his nose.

Molsemis' sister Nolka smiled at Tanial and filled the bowl for him. Nolka was small, maybe nine years old. Smooth black braids brushed her round cheeks. Her dress was neatly fringed and embroidered with porcupine quills, for Nolka was handy with quills. At her belt dangled a small bag, half-embroidered, which she worked on when she had time. Now she had more urgent work to do. "I saw the swan fly over," she told Tanial. "I hoped you would get him." She took the bird away to pluck.

Sitting with Molsemis by the fire pit, Tanial gulped down mush without salt or drippings and found it delicious. Every meal he got Tanial found delicious. Wolfing down mush, he did not notice when the prayer drum fell silent.

The smell of food had drawn Mhlosses out of his spirit tent. He came shuffling to the fire in his tattered French blanket, gripping his bark bowl in trembling claws.

If Tanial sat silent, it might be thought that he feared the old powwow, and Tanial was desperately afraid of being thought afraid. He spoke up boldly, "Ho, Mhlosses! Did the spirits speak to you?"

Mhlosses did not answer at once. First he filled his bowl. Then, swinging his blanket like a royal robe, he turned his weather-carved face upon Tanial. "Yengi Tanial, when the spirits speak to me, you hear them yourself. Did you hear voices? Did my tent bounce about like blown thistledown?"

Tanial had been teasing, but now he felt a troubled disappointment. The evening seemed colder. He asked sadly, "Then you do not know where the hunters are?"

Mhlosses grinned. "I know exactly where they are." He lifted a skinny claw and pointed west.

At the same moment the black dog jumped up. Barking and yipping, the whole pack of lean dogs streamed out of camp toward the west where dark figures moved in darkness.

Tanial's lonely heart leaped. Awasos was coming!

The first hunter to step into the firelight was Awasos' brother, Natanis. Natanis was big and arrow straight. Hawk feathers sprouted in his braids. A French musket leaned like a friend on his shoulder, and on his broad breast jiggled a necklace of amputated fingers. Natanis was tremendously proud of this necklace. Many of the fingers he had chopped off the hands of dead enemies, others he had won gambling. He carried a new knife in his belt. Firelight gleamed on its blade and on his blue-painted cheeks.

After Natanis, Awasos would surely appear. Tanial rose to greet him. But instead came the young men—Azo and Sozap. Tanial looked to see if they carried meat on their shoulders, but they had no burdens. They, too, sported new knives and friendly blue paint, and Sozap wore a battered hat with a white plume.

A shriek shivered the dark, and all the dogs leaped and barked again. The black dog backed against Tanial, stiff hairs rising on its spine.

Tanial had been half-expecting some such joke, but even so his nerves jumped. This sounded like the scream of Real Adders attacking a sleeping camp. Natanis turned a look of cold disapproval upon the screamer, Adagi, who pranced lamely into the light.

Adagi was a little older than Tanial. His narrow eyes gleamed constant fun. He shone like the moon in a white shirt ruffled down the front, and a string of painted bone dice swung at his waist. Adagi pranced because he was Adagi, but he limped under a heavy sack. Tanial smiled at sight of that sack. There must be meat! But where was Awasos?

Katetin asked Natanis. "Awasos?"

Natanis frowned. "Awasos came ahead of us," he told

8

her. "We stopped to trade." He shrugged. "Maybe he went on hunting."

Tanial felt suddenly cold. Breath stuck in his throat. The hunters, gathering about the kettle, gave him sour looks. Natanis, especially, looked at him with frank hate.

To show that he was not afraid, Tanial spoke loudly to Adagi. "Let's see that meat!"

"No meat," Adagi declared cheerfully. "We traded the meat for this." He slung the sack down beside Tanial. Metal jingled inside it. Something shiny fell off the top and grazed Tanial's foot. He looked down at it, unbelieving.

Between two raised platforms ran a long iron blade. At one end the blade curled steeply up, like a ram's horn. Sturdy thong laces trailed from the platforms.

Tanial stooped, picked the thing up, turned it in his hands. Wonder spread like a bright cloud across his mind. First came the south-flying swan and now—a skate.

"That is mine," Adagi reminded him.

"Adagi." False calm softened Tanial's voice. "This thing is worthless by itself. You need two of these." He held his breath.

Adagi kicked the sack. "I have two of them, but I do not know their use."

2) The Winter Maker

I am dreaming and singing in my poor way over the earth;
I who will soon return to earth.

—CHIPPEWA SONG

The Winter Maker, the north wind, came in the night. He howled like a furious ghost, and rattled the bark shingles of the wigwam. His freezing fingers reached under it, lifted and rocked it. Tanial was glad of the warmth of the little black dog, curled under his knees.

The small fire died slowly in the stone circle. Beside Tanial, Nolka lay sleepily fondling her white puppy's ears. With round dreamy eyes she watched Tanial's fingers. He was binding swansdown into a soft ball.

Beyond, Molsemis dozed, hands crossed on his full stomach. Tanial wondered how soon any of them would have a full stomach again. His worrying Yengi blood still made him think like that.

Across the glowing hearth, Katetin stopped snoring. She twitched, rolled over, and moaned. Tanial wondered if she was dreaming of Awasos, somewhere far off in the blowing dark. Not likely. That was his Yengi worry again. Fretting about Awasos would not bring him back. He would come in his own time, like the spring. One lived with what was.

Hunched beside Katetin, old Talaz hissed French prayers. The prayer beads gleamed, slipping through her gnarled fingers. If Talaz would only stop doing that, Tanial thought, Mhlosses might stop hating him. Mhlosses hated the French religion, taught by the black robes, because it scorned his magic. The Yengi religion, he said, was no better. They were very much alike, neither of them respected magic. And Tanial was a Yengi, no one but Awasos ever forgot that.

Adagi said, "You know the use of these things. When will you tell me?" He lay on his back, resting one ankle on his raised knee. One of his new treasures hung by its blade from his big toe.

Tanial grinned. "I will tell you when the time is right."

"And when will that be?"

Tanial glanced up the side of the creaking tent to the dark smoke hole. "The Winter Maker decides that."

"Ah. It must be cold, for these things? They are only good in winter—like snowshoes?"

Tanial winced. Adagi was too near the truth. To change the subject, he asked "What did you trade for them?"

Adagi laughed. "I had nothing to trade. So while the rest of them traded, I took what I liked. One Frenchman talked too fast to notice me. The other saw me, but he never said a word."

"Did you steal the shirt, too?"

"They gave me that. They gave Sozap the hat, too. What bird's feather is on that hat, Tanial?"

Molsemis opened one eye and yawned. "That hat comes from far away," he said. "Maybe from over the water."

The mention of feathers recalled Tanial to his work. He finished bunching the soft down and bound the ball with vine. "Nolka, watch. This is what you do." He batted the

11

rude shuttlecock on his open palm. Slowly it bounced, then sailed high into the dim tent. Nolka smiled.

"Try it tomorrow," Tanial said. "See how far it will go." The shuttlecock drifted down into Nolka's hands. She snuggled against the black dog. He whined and stretched in his sleep.

Outside, the Winter Maker screamed. Near the smoke hole a shingle reared up and flew away, and through the enlarged hole Tanial saw the star bear walking in the sky. Four stars formed the bear. Then came two star Indians tracking him. The second Indian carried a pot—a third star—in which to cook the bear.

"You traded the meat away," Tanial grumbled. "And that was the last of the cornmeal tonight. What are we going to eat tomorrow?"

Molsemis glanced sideways at him. "Your heart is Yengi, Tanial. Worry, worry, worry, about tomorrow. We will have snow by morning. Hunting is easy in the snow."

Adagi swung the shining treasure on his toe. He said, "You are a good shot, Tanial—good on snowshoes, good with everything. You come hunting with us. Much better than sitting hungry in camp!"

Adagi's praise warmed Tanial's heart, but he answered, "Natanis would not let me go."

"Ho!" Molsemis raised on an elbow. "Natanis does not believe in you, Tanial. He thinks you only wait for a chance to run away."

Soberly Tanial asked him, "And what do *you* think?"

"My father, Awasos, believes in you. I believe in you." Molsemis lay down.

Adagi let the treasure slide off his toe. "I think," he mumbled sleepily, "these things are axes. You tie them on your hands. What do the Yengis call them?"

"They are called skates."

"And they are axes, aren't they ?"

"You will have to guess again!"

But Adagi humped over on his side and was silent.

Tanial wriggled down, sharing his warmth with the black dog. He glanced again at the bear in the sky, and wondered if the star hunters wore snowshoes. A cloud swept over the bear, blurring the sky hunt. The sound of snoring merged with wind into silence.

Safe in sleep, Tanial entered his other world, the Yengi world of solid houses, gentle animals, and fine materials. Its people talked loudly, and constantly. (Their name "Yengi" ["The Silent Ones"] was Abenaki wit.) In Tanial's dreams they were giants; for he had been little when he last saw them, and all adults loomed big. They were rough giants, loud, harsh, even to each other. They gave nothing away, even to the needy ones among them. Each family lived in its own closed house, hoarding goods and food to itself. Harsh to themselves, they were bitter enemies to the Abenakis. The Indians were saved only by the Yengis' clumsy ignorance of the forest world. For as Mhlosses said, the Yengis were as many as stars.

Tanial knew all about the Yengis' greed, cruelty and stupidity. The fireside tales he had heard should have hardened him against them. But in his secret heart he longed to see those solid walls again. Love and cheer, he knew, lived within the closed houses. Laughter sounded behind barred doors. Among those loud rough giants he would find his safety . . . if he could ever reach them. Among the generous loyal Abenakis, Tanial still felt like a swan in a flock of ducks. In sleep, he flew away to join his own flock.

This time he whooshed into his secret world on skates!

He swung along over the shining ice, twice as fast as the youngsters around him. For he was back in Penacook. They were all in a race together, and Daniel was winning, as usual. Gracefully outpacing all rivals, he swung down a narrow stretch of ice alone. Forest closed around him, gray and cold and unknown. But there ahead was home, a solid cabin, with smoke rising from its mud-and-stone chimney.

Daniel stood inside the cabin, before the tall stone fireplace. A tame fire hissed quietly, the hanging kettle steamed. Beyond the circle of gentle light was darkness, but Daniel knew the unseen room behind him. He knew where the oak table stood, he knew the settle against the wall, and the ladder to the loft. He knew, too, that the cabin no longer existed. Natanis and others had burned it to the ground. But in the country of sleep, this did not matter. He stood again at his father's hearth.

His older sister Hannah was busy at the fire, her back turned to Daniel. Sunny hair spilled from under her kerchief, and her gray homespun dress glowed rosy in firelight.

She pushed a shovel into her "oven"—a hole in the stones of the fireplace—and lifted out a loaf of steaming bread. Daniel had not seen or tasted bread in years. Somehow, dreaming, he actually smelled the bread.

Hannah turned to him and spoke in English, a language he had forgotten, which came back to him only in dreams. "Dan," she said, "God has answered your prayers."

He nodded. "God sent me a south-flying swan. I have a flight feather here in my pouch."

Hannah's eyes flashed blue scorn. "Daniel Abbott, do you think God cares what you have in that filthy pouch, besides fleas?"

"Why, yes, ayah, I think so. Look at this." Daniel lifted the matted warped book from his pouch and held it out to Hannah.

She gasped. "Father's Bible! How did you save that?"

"I didn't save it. Awasos did. Later on he gave it to me. He knew the Yengis valued it." Daniel stuffed the Bible back in his

14

pouch and reached for the bread on Hannah's shovel.

She stepped away, scolding. "How can you think of food, now!"

"Sister, I can always think of food!"

"You're a proper heathen." She leaned toward him and insisted, "But now you must think of nothing but escape. God has sent you the means."

3) Natanis' Necklace

Men who are brave and heroic
As you deem them to be,
Like them I also
Consider myself to be.

—CHIPPEWA SONG

The spirit tent trembled in the snow-whirling morning wind. It jumped and rattled as if a wind answered from inside.

Around the tent the hunters waited. Natanis stood hunched under his blanket on which snow piled like soft fur. Adagi crouched behind him, absently jiggling his painted bone dice.

Tanial fingered the shabby Bible in his pouch. It felt real, firm to his fingers. Snow whirling in his eyes dizzied him, mutterings and squeals from the spirit tent confused him, and the cold emptiness in his stomach was no help. But the Bible was solid, and so was the warmth of the black dog, huddled at his feet.

Now the spirit tent roared and hopped. Inside, hoots and shrieks alternated with the tap of the prayer drum.

Molsemis muttered in Tanial's ear, "After this, Mhlosses will surely find game!"

Tanial whispered back, "I see; I believe." So spoke Daniel

16

Abbott the Yengi. But Tanial the Abenaki waited on frozen feet to hear what the spirits told Mhlosses.

Next to Molsemis, Nolka cuddled her white puppy. She glanced over her shoulder, and Tanial heard her whisper to Molsemis, "Mother is looking for a dog." So there would be something to eat, after all.

The spirit tent leaped, contorted like a dancer, and shuddered to a standstill. For a moment Mhlosses could be heard speaking. Then there was silence.

Natanis stepped forward. Adagi stood up. Tanial saw Azo and Sozap move toward the tent, gray shadows in snow mist.

The deerskin flap was plucked aside, and Mhlosses tottered out. Bent double, he leaned on Natanis and stared about with glazed eyes.

The hunters closed in about him. When Molsemis moved closer, Tanial followed. Whatever Molsemis did, he did too. That way he could be sure he would never act the slave's part.

Mhlosses pointed east. He quavered, "Moose."

"How many?" Natanis asked. Mhlosses' head and hands shook. "Moose," he insisted, "close to shore. His track is on the shoreline." With a feeble finger, he pointed east again and again.

The hunters' somber faces relaxed. Smiles flashed. Natanis decided, "We go when the storm ends." Gently he set Mhlosses back upright, and turned away.

Turning, he came face to face with Molsemis and Taniel. "My nephew," he said to Molsemis, "come hunting with us." Blanket billowing in the snowy wind, Natanis strode off to the wigwams. Molsemis gazed after him, his face radiant with glad surprise. "I am going moose hunting!" he murmured. "My father Awasos will come back and eat *my* moose!" He swung around and headed for the wigwams and his store of arrows.

Tanial stood alone in the dizzying snow. Natanis had not looked at him.

"Molsemis!" He started after his friend. Behind him, the black dog yelped.

Tanial whirled. Big Katetin had the dog by the tail. The twisting snarling dog could not get a grip on her fist. She jerked the dog off balance and hauled it away backward. Nolka stood frozen, hugging her puppy.

Squealing, the black dog vanished in the snow mist. Tanial felt its squeal like a cry for help. He moved to follow Katetin; then he paused.

Katetin had picked out his dog friend as the least useful dog in the pack. There was only one other less useful—that was Nolka's puppy.

Standing undecided, Tanial heard a screech and a thump. That settled the matter. He knew that he would eat the black dog as readily as the others did. Without too much trouble he pushed the whole business down out of sight in his mind. Well he knew how to push thoughts down and let them sleep!

"Molsemis!" he called and ran after his friend.

Molsemis had reached the wigwam curtain. Tanial ran up and whispered, "I am coming, too!"

Molsemis' jaw dropped, slightly. "Did Natanis tell you so?"

"No, Molsemis. *You* will tell *him.*"

"You want me to tell Natanis—" Troubled, Molsemis thought it over. He glanced sideways at Tanial, then into the wigwam. Having decided, he faced Tanial squarely. "Even Adagi said you should go hunting! Come, brother. We will talk with Natanis."

The smoke inside the wigwam was as blinding as the

snow outside. Tanial winked and blinked, and finally saw the hunters.

Cross-legged, straight-backed, Natanis sat by the hearth. His corncob pipe filled the air with the rich scent of tobacco. Even smelling the smoke eased Tanial's hunger. Smoking, he knew, could almost make you forget hunger.

Across the hearth, Azo and Sozap passed a clay pipe back and forth. Adagi sat daringly close to Natanis. He was chewing pitch gum. He shot a bright questioning look at Molsemis and Tanial. No one else seemed to see them.

Molsemis stood before Natanis, as straight as he could stand under the pitched roof. He cleared his throat and said too loudly, "My uncle."

Natanis looked up.

Molsemis repeated, "My uncle." He seemed to take courage from those words. "You invited me to hunt with you."

Natanis blinked. Across the hearth, Azo and Sozap blew smoke rings and watched.

Molsemis went on more boldly. "Here is my brother, Tanial Waligit. His skill is equal to mine."

"Equal," Tanial thought, "equal? I can split his arrow on the target, and he knows it!" Adagi's eyes glinted. He knew it, too.

"We have waited long for the day when we could hunt together," Molsemis declared. "Let my brother come hunting, uncle. Together we will bring down your moose."

Natanis shifted his gaze to Tanial's face. He blew a smoke ring, and answered Molsemis. "Your brother's eyes are blue as the summer sky."

Adagi stirred and muttered. Finding courage, he said, "Natanis, it is true that Tanial has blue eyes. It is also true that he has a strong bow arm. I would gladly hunt with Tanial Waligit."

19

Across the hearth, Sozap and Azo blew smoke rings and watched.

Molsemis said too loudly, "Let my brother show us that his blue eyes lie."

Before he could stop himself, Tanial clenched his fists. "My eyes do *not* lie," the gesture said. "I am a Yengi."

Silently Natanis noted this. He said to Molsemis, "Hunters often may become separated, each one by himself. Leave Tanial Awakon in camp with Katetin. Then you will be sure to find him again."

Desperately Molsemis argued. "Tanial will not run away. My father, Awasos, believes in Tanial. If he were here, Tanial would hunt."

Natanis agreed. He smiled, and remarked, "My brother Awasos is *not* here." Drawing on his pipe, he seemed to forget the boys standing before him.

For a long moment, Tanial watched the proud hunter smoking as though he were alone in the wigwam. Natanis shut his eyes and tipped his head back. Against his dark pulsing throat stirred his most prized possession—the necklace of amputated fingers.

Tanial spoke up softly. "Natanis, I will gamble with you."

At the word "gamble," Natanis opened his eyes. Adagi sat up straighter; Moslemis turned startled eyes on Tanial. Across the hearth, Azo and Sozap blew smoke rings and watched.

Natanis stretched lean lips into a grin. "Tanial Awakon," he taunted, "you have nothing to wager!"

Tanial could not accept that name—"slave." His life depended on his never accepting it. He swallowed and said quickly, "I will wager you a finger."

20

4) Red Snow

Hark how the thickets snap!
Fearless the footfalls pass
Pushing the trees apart,
Great horns dividing them.
                    —IROQUOIS SONG

The dogs ran first into gray morning light. Brown and white and spotted dogs bounded east along the lake shore, and scampered over new uncertain ice. Their barks drifted back to the hunters following.

"How are we going to hunt," Tanial asked Molsemis, "with all this noise?"

Adagi laughed. "They will not bark for long," he assured Tanial. "Now they are happy to be hunting. Later, they will be quiet."

Tanial struggled over a drift. He had taken Awasos' snowshoes, which were too large for him. Already his back ached.

"I am going on the ice," he told Molsemis. "No snowdrifts there."

Molsemis did not think the ice was strong enough. Tanial was not sure about this, either, but when he stepped away from the shore, the ice did not crack.

"It's thick," he called to Molsemis. He untied the snow-shoes, slung them on his back, and hurried after the dogs. The morning whitened as Tanial trotted eastward. Over-hanging trees bowed under a weight of fuzzy snow, hemlocks on a hillock lifted snowy arms against the brightening sky. Hearing light footsteps, Tanial glanced back. Molsemis was trotting close behind.

Adagi and the others snowshoed along the bank. Tanial could not see them through the screen of snow-piled brush, but he heard the click and creak of snowshoes. Natanis' commanding voice echoed once against the lakeside trees. At the sound Tanial shivered and glanced at his hand—by nightfall the third finger might well be missing.

"Tanial." Molsemis came up beside him. "What do you have to do to keep your finger?"

"I have to be there when they kill the moose."

Molsemis looked relieved. "You do not have to kill the moose yourself?"

"No, only to be there, on top of him."

Molsemis trudged beside Tanial in thoughtful silence. As Adagi had predicted, the dogs were now silent. Tanial glimpsed them ahead, brown and white streaks dodging from ice to the bank and back. The creak of snowshoes on shore mingled with the thud of snow, falling from shaken brush.

Molsemis said suddenly, "I think you have made a foolish wager. Natanis wins either way. If you are not there with the moose, he takes your finger. He would like to take your scalp, too. He is waiting for you to run away."

"I know that." Tanial thought briefly of the flight feather in his pouch.

"If you are there with the moose, Natanis loses nothing by it. But you anger Sozap and Azo, and even Adagi."

"Anger them?" Tanial was truly puzzled. "Why should they be angry?"

"You always win, Tanial. Nobody likes one who always wins."

Tanial had not thought of that. Until now he had survived by winning. The more the Indians admired him, the less they hated him. But he saw now that he could go too far. He strode along briskly enough, but his heart seemed to be sinking slowly into his stomach.

"Why did you insist on hunting?" Molsemis wanted to know.

"Because Natanis called me slave."

"You were right to insist." Molsemis smiled.

Sometimes, with Molsemis, Tanial felt a gentling warmth. He felt it with Nolka, too, and most of all with Awasos. Tanial paused and looked back toward the distant camp. He half hoped that Awasos might be in sight, plodding after them. But the ice stretched away empty, cold green in the white light.

"Come," Molsemis urged. "The others are going inland."

He bounded up the bank, stooped, and laced on his snowshoes.

Tanial followed. Ahead the crunch of snowshoes was fast growing faint. Fighting through a hemlock thicket, he got snow down his neck at every step. When he broke through into open woods, Molsemis was studying the tangle of snowshoe tracks.

"They are going inland," he said thoughtfully. "But Mhlosses said the moose would be close to shore."

"Do what you like, Molsemis. I am staying with the others. I have to be there!"

"Wait." Molsemis held up a hand. "All you can do now is to follow their tracks. You would get there too late. But if we follow the shore, I think we will get there first."

Tanial sighed. "You sound sure that there's a moose!"

"If there is not, you will keep your finger. If there is, he is very likely to be close to shore."

Molsemis' reasoning made sense. Like his little cousin the deer, the moose was very fond of water. The Winter Maker would send him inland and uphill later, but this was only the first snowfall. Tanial clenched his third finger on his bow and said, "You lead."

At noon, color swept over the world. Tanial saw the snow suddenly dazzle, the oaks and maples glow orange, but he was too tired to understand it. Exhausted, he leaned against a shining oak while Molsemis puzzled over the snow beyond.

"Here's the sun," Molsemis remarked. Then Tanial recognized it. It was the first sunshine in many days.

He asked hopelessly, "Any tracks?"

"Not a snowshoe track." Molsemis laughed.

"*Any* track?"

"Yes." Molsemis' voice had a happy teasing ring. "I see here a partridge track. He would make a tasty snack!"

Tanial tucked his third finger into his palm. "Molsemis," he warned, "we have no time for that."

"Something else—moose tracks."

Tanial pushed himself away from the trunk of the oak and went to see. The hoof prints were huge. Pointed like deer tracks, they were larger than the cattle tracks he remembered from Penacook. Though the snow was deep, the tracks were clear with few scuff marks.

"See how high he steps," Molsemis murmured, pointing.

Tanial set off along the tracks. He kept well to the side, and held his bow ready. Molsemis creaked up behind him

and laughed in his ear. "No need for such caution, Tanial.
He's far ahead."

"How can you tell that?"

"See the snow in the tracks. It's dull, stale. When we come
near the moose, the fresh snow will sparkle."

Tanial nodded, understanding. The snow in the huge
tracks did have a settled look. But the tracks could not be
very stale; the storm had ended only last night. Since then,
the moose had passed here.

Farther on, Molsemis commented, "It's a bull."

Again Tanial had to ask respectfully, "How do you
know?"

Molsemis pointed at two birches, leaning close together.
The moose had detoured. "He could not pass between. His
antlers are too wide."

As they followed the tracks eastward, the brief winter sun
began to sink. Their lengthening shadows turned purple.
The moose had walked over a stand of saplings, bending
them double. He had stripped bark from one side of each
sapling with his teeth. Beyond the saplings he had turned
abruptly inland.

"He turns," Molsemis breathed. "And see, the tracks
shine." The hoof marks sparkled fresh. "He is going to rest,
so he turns downwind. Quick, out of the wind!"

Molsemis led Tanial north across the tracks, then south
again, meeting and crossing the tracks. Puzzled, Tanial
pushed wearily over the snow, following Molsemis' determined lead. For Molsemis seemed to know what he was
about. Now he held his bow ready, and glanced alertly
ahead into the deepening shadows. Five times he led Tanial
across and beyond the tracks. Then he stopped, took off his
snowshoes, and slung them on his back.

Tanial stepped off his snowshoes into knee-deep snow.

Sharp pains shot up his legs and spine. Molsemis gestured, and pressed on. They stepped high, like moose themselves, trying not to crunch.

Molsemis crouched. Tanial dropped down close to his shoulder. He was almost too tired to remember why they were here, hunkered together in a hemlock stand on a cold evening. His aching back held most of his attention. Absently biting his third finger, he remembered.

Gently he pushed down the hemlock bough from his face. Beyond was a small clearing, orange in sunset. In the glowing snow rested a vast shadow.

The bull lay quietly. He was just lifting his head, the shadows of his sweeping antlers bridged the small clearing. There was about him a strong odor, oddly comforting, an odor of warm, mossy breath and sweaty hide. There was also about him a calm, a peaceful contentment that Tanial could feel even through his own excitement. The moose was perfectly content and at home in the snow. He lived in contentment, broken only by rare moments of danger. Surrounded by a wolf pack, he might react with fear and anger. Once the danger was past, he would forget it. He never worried about the future. He was not worried now, only puzzled. Grunting, he reared up out of the snow.

Tanial felt Molsemis beside him raise his bow. As the bull rose, he brought up his own bow. His hands shook. The looming bull was peering into the hemlocks with small, golden-brown eyes. Under the heavy antlers his ears flipped and twitched. His hairy nostrils expanded. Uncertain where danger might lie, he turned his side, a breathing wall, to the hemlocks.

"He won't charge," Tanial told himself firmly. "He's just a deer giant; that's all he is." It was hard to believe. The stamping, twitching moose looked like three Penacook dairy bulls. Out of Tanial's dim Yengi memories rose the words

Behemoth and Leviathan.

"I'm not afraid of a deer!" He said it aloud and let fly. It was not possible to miss. Tanial's black-rimmed arrow sank into the breathing wall below the shoulder. At the same moment Molsemis' red-rimmed arrow struck among the ribs.

The bull jerked around, facing the hemlocks. For a frozen, stupefied moment, Tanial thought he would run them down. He shook his enormous head. Hackles bristled on his neck. The snow beneath him darkened, red-spattered. He wheeled sideways again, and Molsemis loosed a second arrow.

The bull thundered forward. Even now he picked his hoofs up high, stepping grandly. Even now his tracks were clear, barely scuffed. But he left a trail of blood splashes, heavier at each step.

Molsemis leaped up to follow.

"Wait!" Tanial cried. "Let him think he is safe!" His father had told him about deer hunting. A wounded deer should be let alone; then it would lie down. Pursued, it would run for miles.

But it seemed a moose was different. Molsemis called over his shoulder, "He will run anyhow!"

Tanial slung his bow behind and slogged after Molsemis.

Uproar broke out ahead. Somewhere past birch and elder thickets, dogs barked and bayed. Sozap shouted; Azo answered. Tanial pushed ahead faster, fighting through windfalls and drifts. He gasped to Molsemis, "Can't see!"

"No matter," Molsemis panted. "Go downhill." Tanial understood promptly. The moose was making for the lake.

The uproar rose and fell like a storm. Now the boys were close enough to hear the crunch of snowshoes as the hunters converged on the lake.

Tanial pushed through a thicket and came out on the bank. The lake shone under a full, rising moon. Not far out, the dogs milled about a vast hulk. A path of broken ice and black water led out to the dead bull. He lay half in water, half on ice, one antler jutting up like the bough of a felled tree.

The hunters slid, snowshoes rasping, out from the bank, and kicked the dogs away.

Molsemis and Tanial crossed the ice. Natanis turned on them. Even in the pale moonlight, Tanial saw the triumph in his face. He thought the triumph was for the moose, because they had food.

But Natanis shouted, "Tanial Awakon, where were you?"

Tanial stopped. Azo and Sozap laughed. Natanis left the moose and pushed toward Tanial. As he came, he drew his new French knife.

Molsemis cried, "Uncle, that is Tanial's moose!"

Natanis paused. Molsemis ran up to the moose and pointed to the three bristling arrows.

"These two are mine," he declared. "They are red. This black one is Tanial's. This arrow hit first."

The young men murmured. Very slowly Natanis slid the knife back in his belt, and Tanial folded his third finger into his palm.

Adagi laughed. "Then Tanial gets the muffle! This is his first hunt, and *he* gets the muffle!" Adagi's laughter doubled him up. No one else laughed. And Tanial remembered Molsemis' warning, "Nobody likes one who always wins."

Adagi untied and kicked off his snowshoes. "Come, there will be a bit left for the rest of us. Look Tanial. I brought a skate. It's a fancy skinning knife, see?"

He held up the skate. Moonlight shivered down the long blade. Tanial looked at the shining blade, and then at Adagi's determinedly good-natured face. Then he looked at

the hating faces around him. Azo and Sozap regarded him
with cold dislike. Natanis raised his chin skyward. This gesture he shared with his brother Awasos.

With all his heart Tanial longed for Awasos. For an instant he seemed to feel Awasos' kind hand on his shoulder,
but it was only Adagi's hand.

Adagi pushed by, going to the moose. The skate he held
reflected white moonlight. The blade flashed in Tanial's eyes
like a signal.

5) The Ice Dance

I make those brave men dance, every one of them!
—CHIPPEWA SONG

"Now," Tanial said, "You go."

"Go where?" Adagi lifted a hand to shade his eyes from the noonday sun.

"On the ice. Now I will show you the use of your skates."

"Ho!" Interest brightened Adagi's sleepy face. He sat up, and clapped a hand on his drum-tight stomach.

Tanial laughed. "If you fall on the ice, you can roll!"

Adagi grumbled. "Have you not eaten, Tanial?"

Waddling past, Katetin answered him. "Tanial stowed meat away in his pouch, like a selfish Yengi. But I caught him at it."

Tanial blushed. Katetin had indeed caught him red-handed, stuffing meat in his pouch instead of sharing it with the others. He was Abenaki enough to feel ashamed.

Katetin waddled over to the fire and sat down by Talaz. The old woman suffered with a bad tooth. Katetin tore and chewed meat for her. She popped the softened meat into

Talaz's mouth with the delicate motion of a robin feeding its young.

Nearby Nolka sat stuffing herself and her puppy. The white puppy lay in her lap like a baby, paws waving over its round, packed stomach.

Too full to talk, the others lay propped against trees and hillocks. From the fire came a rich smell of grease and meat. The moose intestine, stuffed with grease, hung looped over the fire. The sizzle of splashing, burning fat was music to the camp.

Only the dogs, and Tanial, were alert. The dogs circled the feast at a cautious distance, waiting the right moment to dart in and grab. Tanial had eaten sparingly, only enough to strengthen him for what he had finally decided to do.

"Why show me now?" Adagi protested, as Tanial pulled him to his feet.

"Now is when you do it. This is a fun thing, a Yengi game. Come, bring the skates."

With an insistent hand at Adagi's elbow, Tanial guided him down to the ice. Nolka looked up as they passed. Molsemis and Natanis rolled over and struggled to their feet. One by one, the stuffed feasters ambled down to the lake.

Tanial slid the skates onto Adagi's feet. He tied the laces, not too firmly, and stood back.

"These are like Manibozo's magic moccasins," he explained. "One step carries you ten."

Adagi looked doubtfully from the pale green ice to the skates on his feet. "You do not joke?"

Tanial kept his face solemn. "Would I fool you, Adagi? Believe me, the Yengi can do this. I think maybe even the French can do it!"

Adagi tried to stand away from the bank. The skates slipped under his pushing feet. Tanial reached a hand, saying, "Everyone needs a little help at first." He grasped

31

Adagi's elbow, and yanked.

"*Oof!*" Adagi clung to Tanial as the skates slipped wildly about.

Tanial chuckled. "You, Adagi, are strong and witty. You will learn this sport fast. You will fly like a bird." He shoved Adagi off and away.

Speeding over the ice, Adagi bent double and flailed his arms. His ankles wobbled and folded, and he crashed down in a heap.

Laughter cackled from the bank. Tanial glanced back and saw Big Katetin shaking and shrieking. Beside her, Nolka smiled. Natanis came stepping down the long bank, tilting his head back and smiling from a noble distance.

Adagi growled. Resting his weight on his open palms, he flailed his feet but could not rise.

Tanial walked over to him. "Once more," he said brightly. "Try again, graceful Adagi. Look, I will start you off." He grabbed Adagi under the arms and hoisted him up. "Keep your feet straight under you," he advised kindly. "Push with this foot, lean on that one. Ready."

"*Augh,*" said Adagi, and Tanial shoved him off. Again Adagi crashed like a sack of acorns, flung down on the ice.

Natanis cast off his blanket and stepped onto the ice. "I see what Adagi does wrong," he declared. "I will wear those skates myself and show him."

"Ho!" cried Adagi, "ho, ho! Yes, indeed!" He seemed glad to let Tanial unlace the skates and remove them from his feet. Rubbing his hip, he stood by while Natanis sat on the ice and firmly fastened the skates to his own feet.

"Help me stand," he ordered Tanial, who leaped to help him.

Natanis leaned for an instant on Tanial's shoulder. "*Hm,*" he said to himself, trying out the ice with cautious slides.

"Hm, hm." He took a deep breath, pushed away from Tanial, and sailed off.

For a moment it looked as though Natanis might skate. He had figured out Adagi's trouble with his ankles. He held his own ankles stiff as boards, also his knees. After three stunted steps, he toppled backward. His head thudded on the ice.

Tanial stood transfixed. If Natanis were injured, he was to blame. On the bank, laughter died. Dogs growled. Azo and Sozap came running, thumping the ice.

Natanis rolled over on his stomach. He looked up and grinned, and Tanial breathed again. Katetin shrieked with laughter. Sozap and Azo gabbled together.

Tanial felt a light touch on his arm. Molsemis stood beside him. Tanial shot him a grin, and a challenge. "Will you try it, Molsemis?"

Molsemis mumbled, "Brother, do not anger them."

Tanial looked at him again. Molsemis' eyes were serious. Natanis sat up and untied the skates. "This is not for me," he decided. "One might do it, after much trying. What good would it do?"

One hand pressed to his hip, Adagi stepped forward. He said angrily, "Tanial is fooling us. This is not the real use of the skates."

"Maybe," Sozap agreed. "But I will try. I think if Natanis had leaned forward, he might not have fallen."

So Sozap tied on the skates and scrambled around, leaning far forward and working his arms. He took three falls, then gave the skates to Azo. Five growling dogs chased Azo, snapping at his amazing movements.

Azo had decided that the secret lay in constant motion. He waved, wagged, wiggled, and flopped. He lay panting on the ice.

Big Katetin could hardly catch breath from laughing to
laugh again. Mhlosses and Talaz clung together, weak with
laughter.

Natanis kicked the dogs off Azo, and turned on Tanial.
"Adagi is right.This cannot be the use of the skates! Tell us
the truth!"

"But this is the truth!" Tanial looked from Natanis' stern
face to Adagi's harsh smile to Molsemis' troubled eyes.
None of them believed him! Hope swelled his heart. He
went on, "I have seen the Yengis skate. They fly like birds. I
myself—" He checked himself. Better not to say that he
himself had flown faster than any.

"Ho!" Adagi snatched up the skates, held them out to
Tanial. "Show us!"

"Show them, Tanial," Nolka chirped. She stood with
Molsemis, watching the doings with bright, round eyes. Up
on the bank Katetin nodded, her face one wrinkled grin.
Mhlosses wheezed, "Show us!"

Tanial sat down. He pressed a skate to his right foot and
laced the thongs up around his calf. While he tied on the left
skate, the watching crowd fell silent. He looked up and saw
them looming over him, eager and intent.

Kneeling to rise, he dug the sharp toe of his right blade
into the ice. The left blade pointed straight ahead—south.
Power surged into his legs. Before him stretched smooth ice.
He could start off low and fast. One quick push, one strong
sweep, would carry him out of reach. The crowd did not suspect him.

Or did they? Tanial glanced up again at the dark watching faces. He knew all of them well. A few of them he called
his friends. Now, suddenly, they were aliens. He had first
seen Natanis in the light of his burning home. Natanis' shirt
and hands had been greasy with Tanial's brother's blood.
He had seemed no stranger then than at this moment.

These surrounding strangers were Tanial's enemies, but they did not yet know this. At his first strong motion they would suspect. At his second powerful swing, they would leap to attack. He imagined himself stumbling, and felt Natanis' ax in his head.

No, they stood too close around. Over the years, Tanial might have lost the skill and speed that all Penacook had admired. Better first to try the skates out.

"Look how Tanial starts," Adagi muttered. "He made us stand up."

Slowly, arms fluttering, Tanial drew himself upright. He wobbled his ankles and knocked his knees. And all the while, power surged through him. His feet knew the way south. His thighs ached to push and stretch. But, using perfect control, he wobbled, jerked, wriggled, and sprawled.

"Ha, ha!" Adagi roared with glee. "Tanial cannot do it himself!"

Molsemis said quietly, "If Tanial cannot, no one can."

Sozap asked half angrily, "So you were fooling us?"

"No." Tanial knelt up and rubbed his side, which really did hurt. "I have seen it done, but that was long ago. Perhaps I have forgotten something. Or those skates are missing something."

"Ho, ho!" Natanis grinned down at Tanial. "That must be it—the skates are wrong!" With a gesture he invited laughter from the crowd. Abruptly he turned toward the shore. "I am going to eat."

Mention of eating thinned the crowd immediately. Natanis strode off to the fire. Katetin followed. Azo and Sozap bounded like bucks up the bank, the dog pack playing around them.

But Mhlosses hobbled up to Tanial, and stooped to peer into his face. Tanial hardened his mind. What if the pow-wow could read his thoughts? He was relieved when

35

Mhlosses only shook his head and muttered, wrapped his blanket tighter, and moved away.

Nolka stood watching Tanial. She looked thoughtful, almost mournful. Tanial thought, "If anyone suspects, it is Nolka." But how could she?

Molsemis gave Tanial a strange, secret look. He turned and followed the others, not looking back, and Nolka went with him.

Strangely, Adagi remained. He should have been first back at the food! Tanial waited for him to turn his back. "When Adagi has gone ten steps," he thought, "I'll take off." But Adagi came toward him, instead. "Give me my skates," he said.

Surprised, Tanial protested, "But they are no use!"

"I will find a use. They will make good axes."

There was no help for it. Tanial untied the skates and stood up on the ice in his moccasins. He felt like a bird that lights on the ground.

Adagi set off for the shore, a skate under each arm. Tanial followed, hypnotized by the skates. Now that he had felt their power, he knew that escape was possible. And, as someone had told him in a dream, he could think of nothing else.

6) Flight

It is God that girdeth me with strength,
And maketh my way perfect.
He maketh my feet like hind's feet. . . .
                              —PSALM 18:32–33

"Adagi," Tanial said, "I will gamble with you."

Adagi shook his gambling bowl lazily up and down. The bone dice rattled. Sozap got up and went away, leaving Adagi his bow.

"I am not going to wager this bow," Adagi said.

"I do not want the bow," Tanial assured him. "I have nothing to wager against it. I'll gamble for those—those useless things." He pointed to the skates, standing on their blades in the snow.

"Oh, yes. The Yengi toys." Adagi looked thoughtfully up at Tanial. Blue birch shadows slanted across his face. He sat at the foot of a giant silver birch a little away from the feast. His eyes narrowed. "What have you to wager, Tanial?"

Crouching, Tanial held his bark bowl under Adagi's nose. A rich, hot steam curled up from the white stew in the bowl. "My share—the muffle."

Adagi's nose twitched greedily.

37

A shadow hung over Tanial. Molsemis stood behind him. Tanial glanced up at him carelessly, hiding annoyance. He was beginning to feel hounded by Molsemis.

"You never had muffle before," Molsemis remarked. "Are you sure you want to gamble it away for . . . toys?"

"He wants the toys for remembrance," Adagi sneered.

"Well, I would not mind a dish of muffle! And I will not lose the skates, either. How many throws?" He rattled his dice.

Tanial held up three fingers.

Nolka slipped up behind Adagi. She leaned against the silver birch and watched the jumping dice. For once, her small hands were idle. The half-embroidered bag dangled from her wrist.

Adagi tossed the dice out on the snow. Everyone leaned to see the number that fell uppermost.

"Three!" Tanial laughed. That should be easy to beat. He rolled five.

Behind him he heard the noise of the feast. Fat dropped, hissing, into the fire. Men laughed and joked. Katetin and Talaz talked softly together. Tanial found himself listening for one absent voice. "If Awasos comes even now," he thought, "I will not go."

"Seven." Adagi grinned, scooped up the dice, and dumped them back in the bowl.

"*Oo-oo,*" Nolka mourned. A look from Molsemis hushed her.

Tanial shook the dice. He wondered sadly what Awasos would think when he returned, and found his "son" gone.

"Six." Adagi leered. "I can taste that muffle now." He grabbed back the dice and shook them mightily. He rolled five.

Shaking the bowl for the last throw, Tanial prayed. He had a notion that his father's God should be addressed in English, but he remembered no English except bits of song

and poetry. Silently he recited words he no longer understood. "Hear the right, O Lord; attend unto my cry."

He dropped the dice on the snow: seven. Tanial tasted
blood. He had bitten his tongue.

Adagi snatched up the dice and bowl. Leaping up, he
stalked away. Molsemis called after him, "Adagi, your
bow!"

Muttering, Adagi came back for the bow he had won
from Sozap. When he had gone to the fire, Molsemis
laughed. "I wonder what Adagi would have done if he had
been *hungry!* He wanted that muffle!"

"You eat it," Tanial said absently. He was looking at his
skates.

"What?" Molsemis' astonished voice brought Tanial back
to attention. This would never do! He must not seem too in-
terested in the skates.

"Let's have that muffle!" Tanial crammed a steaming
handful into his mouth, then handed the bowl to Molsemis.

All the stories about moose-muffle were true. Tanial had
never tasted anything so good as this white, chickeny stew.
But while he and Molsemis and Nolka wolfed the luscious
stew, he kept glancing at the skates. The sun flamed on their
blades.

The muffle finished, Tanial wiped his greasy hands on the
snow and stood up. "Is it true," he asked Molsemis, "that
you can travel three times farther on moose meat than on
any other meat?"

Molsemis licked his fingers, nodding. "Moose is very
strong. Now, *we* are very strong."

"Mmm. For another muffle I would run all day, kill another moose. Maybe tomorrow."

"Tomorrow," Molsemis agreed.

Carelessly, as though thinking about something else,
Tanial picked up the skates he had won. He slung them over

his shoulder and went away into the woods.

Gray curtains of forest closed between himself and the feast. Sunshine gleamed green and orange on the trees. Blue shadows crisscrossed sparkling snow. Behind Tanial flowed the rich smell of roasting meat, and the friendly sound of laughter. Before him the woods dipped, blue and white, to the expanse of sun-jeweled ice.

Tanial slipped a hand into his pouch and felt the swan's flight feather. Under it, his fingers found his father's Bible. "Heavy," he thought, and began to draw it out of the pouch. "Better not be weighed down with that!" Then he hesitated. Yengi Daniel wanted to throw the Bible away for the sake of lightness and speed; Abenaki Tanial held onto it, and finally pushed it back into the pouch. It had its own magic power.

"God will give me feet like deer's feet," he said aloud. Some such charm was written in the Bible, he remembered. He patted the Bible down in the pouch, leaped like a deer, and bounded down to the ice.

In a willow thicket at the lake's edge he sat down and laced on the skates. He worked fast and tied the thongs very tightly. As he had told Adagi, it was like putting on magic moccasins. Instantly his feet felt power. "The wind will carry me home," he sang happily to himself, "whenever I have a mind to go. Which is now!"

Snow crunched behind him. Tanial froze. Maybe whoever it was had not seen him. Snow crunched again, nearer.

If they asked what he was doing, he could say he wanted to try this foolishness once more. Then he could put on the ice dance again.

Close behind him, he heard a whisper. "Tanial."

He whirled. Nolka stood among the willows.

Tanial looked earnestly into her round, dark face. He hoped he was seeing her for the last time, but he wished her well. He wished for Nolka to grow up strong and skillful, to marry a good hunter and raise healthy children. He wanted for Nolka the best of her world. But for himself he wanted an entirely different, almost forgotten world. And right now, one cry from Nolka could shatter all worlds for him.

Nolka was silent. Silent, Tanial watched her. She looked at the skates bound so firmly on his feet. She looked at his tense poise, the poise of a bird lifting its wings to air. Still silent, she reached a hand to him. From her scarred and stubby fingertips dangled the little, half-embroidered bag.

Tanial took the bag. It was hot and lumpy. A rich smell of meat wafted up from its gathered opening. He tied it to his waistband.

Voices sounded from the forest-screened camp. Snow crunched as many feet hurried toward the lake. Natanis called, "Tanial, bring the skates! We will dance the ice dance again!"

From the forest, Sozap called, "Tanial is gone! Here are running tracks!"

A screech from Katetin drowned out Natanis' answer. "I told you! I knew! And you fools wanted him to be my son!" She gasped curses as she galloped toward the lake.

Close at hand, Adagi shouted, "Look on the ice, brothers!"

There was no hope now of pretending innocence. Tanial's enemies had awakened from their dream of friendliness. They knew he had turned his back on them.

Still, he hesitated. He looked into Nolka's eyes, trying to show thanks and well-wishing. Then he turned to the lake. He crouched, kicked hard against the bank, and swooped out on the ice.

As a swan rises from the water, it pumps its wings vigorously. Pumping and paddling, it scrambles from water to air. So Tanial pumped and scrambled, jabbing the ice with frantic blades.

The ice groaned, and shifted under the weight of running men. Closer came their whooping shouts; something whistled. Tanial ducked. An arrow zipped over his shoulder and skittered across the ice.

The arrow hit a bump and stopped, almost under his blade. Tanial gathered himself and leaped across both bump and arrow. Landing on his feet, he struck out again at top speed.

"I'm a perfect target," he realized. He was traveling very fast but in a straight line. He dodged toward the bank. Willows leaned out over the ice, cattails spiked the shoreline. A second arrow zinged over Tanial's back and tangled in willow branches.

"That's better," he thought. "Tricky shooting." He zigzagged to make it trickier.

On his left, the bank drew back. A small cove opened here, out of sight of the crowd. As he whooshed around the bend into the cove, Tanial shot a glance over his shoulder.

He took in the scene in a flash, between one swinging step and the next, but he never forgot it. This last image of his enemy friends was seared on his mind as though by lightning.

They were much farther behind than he had dared to hope. He was out of arrow range.

Natanis stood erect with folded arms. The feathers stood unruffled in his hair. Outwitted, he had not lowered himself to the contest. Tanial was fortunately too far away to see his expression, but he knew that the mouth was compressed and the grim eyes smoldered. The long, dark face was tipped up and back, impassive as stone.

Two figures wriggled flat on the ice. Sozap and Azo had tried to run after Tanial. Probably they had hoped he might stumble.

Two bowed, lumpy figures clung together, shaking.

Mhlosses and Talaz had not laughed so hard in years.

Adagi knelt upright. He had shot the arrows Tanial had dodged. Big Katetin now held his bow. She stood over Adagi like a mountain over a wigwam. One large arm aimed the bow which she had just grabbed from his hands. With the other arm she drew the arrow back and back, farther than Adagi could have drawn it. Just as Tanial sped into the cove, she let fly. He was out of range, but Katetin's arrow screeched on the ice at his heels.

Tanial glimpsed one more figure. It was not so much a figure as a motion, coming through the woods. It was Molsemis' somewhat awkward snowshoe stride.

Tanial did not worry. Speeding across the little cove, he laughed to himself. "Ho, Molsemis! You think I will tire? Go chase another moose—that will be easier!" Chuckling, he flew toward the next promontory. The glittering ice sang under his skates. Victory swelled his chest till he had to shout.

"The wind will carry me home!" he yelled into the silence. Hearing his voice, the only sound in the white and sparkling world, he threw back his head and sang. "My music reaches to the sky!" A faint echo returned from the bare trees on the promontory.

Now Tanial was there, skirting the reedy bank. At the tip of the promontory he paused, and spun lightly around to look back. From here nothing could be seen of the camp, or even the camp shoreline. No figures scurried on the ice. The chase had been abandoned.

Tanial swung into a slow easy stride along the shore. He almost struck out across the open lake. Then he realized that he might be seen, alone, in the middle of the bright ice.

And suddenly Tanial shivered. A cloud swept across his mind. His known enemies were far behind, but what of the unknown? The shoreline ahead was willow-bristled, pine-furred. Any bush, any pine, might conceal Indians.

If they were Abenakis, there was nothing to fear. They would know Tanial, Awasos' son. They would invite him to their wigwams and share with him whatever food they had. Even facing starvation tomorrow, they would feed a guest today.

But the shoreline was veering south. This was both encouragement and warning. Home lay south. South, too, lay the country of the Real Adders.

Real Adders constantly snaked about the northern woods. Cold and hunger meant little to them, their endurance amazed even the Abenakis. They would lie in wait near an Abenaki camp for days, hoping to knock some lone hunter on the head. They wanted scalps for glory, and it didn't matter whose scalp. They would gleefully tomahawk tottering old Talaz.

There was no way to guess which thicket hid a Real Adder. Tanial decided he had no choice but to skate along and hope for the best, and a bit of Yengi prayer could not hurt. "The Lord my shepherd is," he sang, "I shall be well supplied ... da-da-da-da, da-da-da-da, What can I want beside?"

He swung slower and slower past overhanging willows. Rounding the tip of the promontory, he saw the whole southeastern curve of the lake, gold-shining. The promontory pines cast a deep blue shadow over the ice. Drifting gently, Tanial felt more and more uneasy.

"I have meat," he thought, touching his pouch. "You can go farther on moosemeat than on any other meat. I have flints to make fire." But he had no blanket. And for the first time he would be alone in the winter night.

"I think," he confessed to himself, "I think I am a little bit afraid. No, no, it is only that my ankles hurt. It is time to stop."

Flight

"Stop!" The shout came from the shadow of a giant pine just ahead. Startled, Tanial glanced sharply up the bank. The shadow moved and shouted again, "Stop!" The voice was weirdly high.

Tanial drew a quick, cold-searing breath. He set toe to ice, ready to strike out, and shoot away.

Out from the shadow came a bow, the arrow notched and aimed. Could he fly faster than the arrow, aimed at close range?

"My arrow is faster than you," the quavering soprano voice answered his thought.

Tanial wobbled and stopped. Tired almost to weakness, he watched his enemy glide out into level light.

7) The Brother

Behold, how good and how pleasant it is for brethren to dwell together in unity!

—PSALM 133:1

He had to bend under a low-swinging branch, but he kept the bow aimed. He wore snowshoes, awkward in that brushy spot. Tanial had suspected whose voice it was, but he was not sure till the enemy slid clear of the pine and stood up straight behind his steady arrow.

Molsemis said, "You are easier to hunt than moose! Why did you follow the shoreline?"

Tanial asked sullenly, "How did you know I would?"

Molsemis crunched closer. "Sure you followed the shoreline," he triumphed, "so as not to be seen by us, or by . . . anyone. I crossed this point while you went around it. You have gone twice as far as I."

Tanial hardly heard Molsemis' talk. Fury and fear made a whirlwind in his heart. Before Molsemis finished his mocking comments, Tanial burst in, "You will not take me back to camp! Try it and see."

Briefly Molsemis' arrow wavered. "I? Take you back to

46

camp? Do you know what would happen then?"

"I tell you, I am not going back." Tanial forced bold words out of a tight throat. Fear stiffened his muscles so that even breathing hurt.

"Brother"—Molsemis dropped his mocking tone—"I am going to lower this arrow. You will not move. You will stand still and listen to me."

Tanial folded his arms and waited. Molsemis lowered his bow, and slipped the arrow into the quiver.

Then quietly Molsemis explained. "I did not come to take you back. I came to show you a good way to go south."

Tanial opened his mouth. No sound came out.

Molsemis continued, "You could follow the shore for days and find no clear way south. I know a river. It will be frozen hard. I know a beaver house. We can camp there a day, catch beavers. You will have plenty of meat then for your journey." Molsemis reached behind him and held up a crumpled blanket. "You will need this."

Tanial trembled. His stomach shook as if he was about to be sick. He waited till the wave of relief ebbed. When he could speak calmly, he said, "Brother, I did not know you."

Molsemis grinned, and relaxed. Then glancing at the sky, he said briskly, "Take off the skates. Walking on the ice, we will leave no track. On that point we will camp." He pointed to a far pine-fringed peninsula.

Tanial took off his skates, and Molsemis removed his snowshoes. Flat on the ice, Tanial's feet prickled painfully. Molsemis, jumping down from the bank, noticed him limping. "No time to rest now," he warned. "Azo and Sozap are not far behind."

Tanial gasped. "But they will be walking on the ice."

Molsemis shook his head, and set off across the ice. "I am like Mhlosses," he said over his shoulder. "I see from far away. I see Azo and Sozap coming now. When you flew around the bend, and they saw you no longer, they came up on the bank. Right away they saw my snowshoe tracks."

"But how would they know? . . . Maybe they thought you had gone hunting."

"Oh, yes." Molsemis laughed. "I go hunting while the full kettle boils! No, Tanial. You did not know me for your brother, but they did. They said, 'Ho! Molsemis goes after his brother.' Then old Talaz said, 'And he has taken my blanket.' Then Azo and Sozap strapped on their snowshoes and came after me. Right now I see them shooshing along on the other side of that neck of land behind us."

Tanial glanced back. Early winter evening was drawing a gray curtain over the ice. No longer sparkling, the ice had a dead green tinge. The pines on the promontory looked black. No creature moved in the gray-green landscape.

"How fast will they cross the neck of land?" Tanial tried to keep his tone matter-of-fact.

Molsemis reassured him. "It will be dark when they come out on shore. They will not see us. We will make our fire inland, where they will not see it. And we leave no tracks."

"What will they do, Molsemis?"

Molsemis chuckled. "They will make fire, eat, sleep. In daylight they will search for tracks. They will say, 'Molsemis and Tanial flew into the sky. The Wendigo carried them off.' " Tanial shivered. The man-eating Wendigo monster seemed suddenly real, and only a little less frightening than the Real Adders.

Gray light sank into darkness. The next point of land was a dark hump against the gray sky. Tanial kept glancing back at the last point. He feared to see two angry shadows scurry out on the ice.

Molsemis spoke without turning. "You look back, Tanial. Do not waste time, stopping to look. Soon it will be dark."
In fact, Molsemis himself was now no more than a moving

shadow. The snowshoes loomed like wings on his shoulders. He set his soft-moccasined feet quietly, firmly, on the smooth ice. Never once did he look back.

Tanial straightened his slumped shoulders and stepped out lightly like his friend. The skates jabbed at his back. "Molsemis," he called softly, "what will you do when you leave me?"

"Go back to camp."

"They will be angry."

After a while, Molsemis answered, "Katetin is my mother. Natanis is my uncle."

"What about Azo and Sozap?" Saying the names, Tanial could not resist a final look behind him. Safe darkness veiled the lake.

"What can they do?" Molsemis pointed out. "Chop a hole in the ice and duck me? I am no longer a little boy!" Thoughtfully, he added, "Coming after you, I saw coon tracks lead into a hollow oak. I will take back a coon for the kettle."

Dark bank, black pines, rose before them. "Now," said Molsemis, "we go inland."

He climbed the bank. Following closely, Tanial pushed and tramped through dark thickets. Often he could not see Molsemis at all. He followed the crunch of snow.

Once he asked, "Is this not far enough?"

"Tanial!" the answer drifted back. "You are fast and strong, but you have no caution."

That was true enough, Tanial thought. No one with an acornful of caution would have tried this skating trick! "Learn caution." Molsemis was scolding like Katetin. "Do you want those who hunt you to see a flicker of firelight?"

"Let's go farther!"

Molsemis laughed and stopped. "This is far enough. Here we are in a hollow."

They dumped snowshoes and skates, and knelt together in the broken crust. Tanial fumbled the flints out of his pouch. Then a grim thought struck him. "Brother, we have no tinder!"

Molsemis heaved a sad sigh. "I said you had no caution. All your strength is in your muscles; your head is weak."

"Stop scolding like a woman! Do you want to freeze?" Kneeling, Tanial was aware of the deepening cold. The fingers that held the flints tingled.

"We will dance," Molsemis answered solemnly. All night we will sing, and dance to our song. That will keep us warm."

Tanial was about to fling out an angry reply, but something in Molsemis' grave tone checked him. He swallowed and said more quietly, "Molsemis. I think you have tinder."

"My head is heavy with wisdom," Molsemis assured him. "Naturally, I have tinder."

Tanial contented himself with one furious snort. For some time they were silent. By turns they struck the cold flints over the heap of dried moss that Molsemis provided. Several sparks lit—feeble stars that fell on snow or died in the air. Tanial's hands and feet grew numb. His nostrils stiffened. At last, a spark lit in the moss and glowed.

"*Hoo-oo. Hoo-ooo.*" Molsemis stretched flat on the snow and blew gently on the moss. The glow deepened and spread. The handful of moss became a miniature forest fire. The strands separated, and blackened like burned trees.

Quickly the boys snatched up twigs and brush, and fed them to the flame. As the fire grew, so grew its light, and more fuel came into view.

"Ho!" said Molsemis when the fire steadied. "That is enough. Pile the rest here. Now we need not dance."

Tanial huddled by the little fire and let its warmth calm

his jumping muscles. Molsemis grinned at him across the flame.

"Now, brother, a bite of moose would warm us all through."

Tanial's spirits rallied quickly with the warmth. "O wise and cautious Molsemis, you brought no meat?"

"I knew you had some, greedy Tanial. I saw you hide it in your pouch."

"You have hawk's eyes, brother."

"I have watched you ever since you saved the swan's flight feather."

Tanial muttered in wonderment. He lifted the little half-embroidered bag and shook scraps of meat into Molsemis' reaching hands. Last, he picked out a small hunk for himself.

Molsemis' eyes glittered at sight of the bag. "That looks like my sister's work."

"You were not the only hawk-eyed spy in camp. Nolka gave me this as I was leaving."

"If my mother hears of that, Nolka will get a ducking!" Chewing, Molsemis looked sideways at Tanial. Several times he took a breath, then let it out silently.

At last Tanial asked, "What is it?"

Molsemis said, "My brother. You see that Nolka loves you, that you and I are good friends." Tanial looked down and fingered the fringe of his shirt. Molsemis went on. "The others were wiser than Nolka and me. They suspected you. But when you killed the moose, they were going to accept you. My mother was almost ready to adopt you. My father has always wanted you for his son." Tanial stared at the toe of his left mocassin. "Why?" Molsemis was asking, "why did you leave us? You have taken a great risk, and made near friends into bitter enemies. Why have you done this?"

Molsemis fell silent. The silence of the dark forest seemed to press in on Tanial's heart. Even the fire whispered. Tanial looked into its flickering heart, where moss and twigs died into embers. In the glowing embers, he saw memory pictures—scenes that had slept in his mind for years now awoke and moved in the flames.

Molsemis waited for his answer. If Tanial kept silence now, Molsemis would not ask again. He would lead him to Beaver River tomorrow, and help him kill beaver. And after that, Tanial knew, he would never see Molsemis again.

He said, "You deserve to know this. Once I had a younger brother. He was four years old. His name was Jamie." Tanial dropped a handful of twigs into the fire, and watched the flames lick them up. Very slowly, haltingly, he told his bitterness to the fire. He seemed to see the story enacted there, red on a black background.

8) Lightning

And they smote all the souls that were therein with the edge of the sword, utterly destroying them: there was not any left to breathe. . . .

—JOSHUA 11:11

A little fire burned on the stone hearth in the cabin. It was early morning in Third Month, and ten-year-old Daniel did not have to open the shuttered window to know that it was still dark outside.

He dressed hastily on the hearthstone, dancing with cold even while he pulled on his pants. The milk pail gleamed in the firelight beside him. It was time to milk Bonny Cow, who lived in the cabin's other room.

Father usually did the milking, but he had gone into Penacook overnight. Sometime today he would be back, with his new bride.

In the meantime Daniel considered himself master of the house. It felt good to be alone and responsible. He was annoyed to hear murmurs and giggles up in the dark loft.

"Want breakfast," Jamie chirped sleepily. "Breakfast first."

"No, sir," came Hannah's crisp voice. "Wash first."

"Icy," Jamie protested.

"Not this morning—I left the pail by the fire. Oh, that reminds me. My bread!"

Straw rustled; the ladder creaked. Daniel turned to see Hannah climbing down from the loft. Her white nightdress drifted, frazzled braids swung. Touching bottom, she ran on swift bare feet across the freezing floor, and peeked into the oven.

"It worked! Look, Dan, it baked overnight." Fourteen years old, Hannah was really in charge of the house. Lifting the baked loaves from the oven, she gave orders. "Hurry the milking, Dan. We have to polish the kettles. And you must make a new broom before—"

"Breakfast first!" Jamie cooed from the loft. Chuckling, he poked his bright head over the edge.

Hannah replied with more commands. "Jamie, come down and wash. Dan, unbolt the door."

Leisurely Daniel stepped into his shoes. "You stop giving orders," he said. Hannah tossed her head, and lifted the lid from the kettle with an important-sounding clang.

And then the world ended.

Daniel would relive the moment in countless dreams. Hannah would clang the lid. Chubby Jamie, struggling with his trailing nightshirt, would climb down the ladder; and Daniel, buckling his belt, would step toward the door.

He was reaching to draw the bolt when the latch wiggled.

He stopped short, staring at the latch. It wiggled soundlessly. Outside, a hand was trying it.

Daniel's insides shrank into a cold hard fist. Watching the jiggling latch, he ran backward to the hearth.

"What in heaven's name—" Hannah began. Daniel clapped a hand on her mouth and nodded toward the door.

He never doubted whose hand tried the latch. As if he

54

could see through the oak door, he knew that an Indian stood outside.

None of them had thought much about Indians before. The wilderness was vast; no Indian trail came near the cabin. Indians were no more likely to strike than lightning, and one does not live in constant fear of lightning. One ignores it—until a thunder storm blows up. Now, without wind or thunder, the storm was upon them.

Jamie reached the floor. Holding up the skirt of his nightshirt with one plump hand, he trotted straight for the shelf of wooden bowls and spoons. His mind was set on breakfast. He never glanced at the hopping latch, but the shelf was near the door.

Hannah tore herself loose from Daniel's grip. She flew across the cabin, past the door, and grabbed Jamie. Jamie let out a startled squawk.

Outside in the morning dark, a hundred roosters crowed. Eerie shrieks froze Daniel's ears. An ax beat the door like a drum. An arrow thudded through a chink in the wall and hung there, caught by its burning feather.

Jamie struggled in Hannah's arms. She rushed him back to the hearth just as a stone ax crashed through the door. She thrust him against Daniel.

She spoke, but Daniel heard no words. She pointed frantically to the cow-shed door, and shoved at him. Then Daniel understood. He was to get Jamie out through there.

Hannah grabbed the iron poker and faced the door. A dark hand pushed in, feeling for the bolt.

The bolt was frozen. That gave Daniel time to drag Jamie into the cow shed. He slammed the door, shutting out the sight of Hannah with the poker.

Later, Daniel comforted himself with the thought that he could not have helped Hannah if he had stayed. But the cold truth was that he had never thought of staying. He had no thought for Hannah, and not much for Jamie. He felt nothing but paralyzing fear.

He bolted the cow-shed door and pulled Jamie through darkness to the outside door. Near but unseen, Bonny Cow lowed and swayed up from her straw bed.

Jamie wept. He cried like a calf, loud and strong. Daniel swung around and cuffed him. "Stop your bawling!" he ordered fiercely. Either because of the blow or the words, Jamie stopped bawling. He hiccuped, and let Daniel pull him along by one limp wrist.

Noise from the main cabin ached in Daniel's head—thuds, hoots, and the voice of rushing fire. The shed door behind him shook and shivered under ax blows.

Daniel yanked Jamie close to him. "Quiet! Don't you make one sound—" He unbolted the outer door and shoved it open.

He glimpsed gray snow, gray sky. Something fell heavily on his shoulder, knocking out his breath. Still gripping Jamie, he collapsed.

He looked straight at a pair of quilled mocassins. Rolling, Daniel saw the stone ax come down. It swung down toward his head in a smooth, swift arc. He had no thoughts about it. Thought and feeling, like breath, had been knocked out of him. Waiting calmly for the ax and his head to meet, he forgot that Jamie was on top of him.

Tanial told Molsemis, "Natanis wore my brother's scalp on his belt till he sold it to the French. I could never forget that. That is why I could never have been your mother's son."

Molsemis nodded and muttered. He tossed a handful of twigs on the dying fire. Warm light played on his grave face.

"You shiver," he said. "Bring your feet close to the fire. If the feet are warm, the body is warm."

Numbly Tanial shoved his feet to the warmth. He still shivered.

Molsemis said, "You and Natanis have long memories."

"Natanis?"

"You have heard how the Yengis burned his wigwam. His wife was inside it."

Slowly Tanial nodded. "I have heard that story."

"That is why Natanis would never have been your uncle. Often he tells this story you have told and with delight. He avenged his wife that day. But I did not know he was talking of you and of your people.

"Tanial, that is all long ago. Your brother Jamie is dead. I, your brother Molsemis, am alive."

Tanial whispered, "That is true."

"Your father has a new wife, maybe new children. Maybe he has forgotten you."

Tanial started. "No! No, that can never happen."

"You were mistaken," Molsemis continued firmly, "to anger your friends and try to go back to the Yengis. The Yengis are not good people. They may treat you badly; their hearts are hard. Among them, you may wish you had never left us."

"They are only people," Tanial murmured. "People like you and Nolka and the rest. Natanis' heart is hard, too!"

"You have made a mistake, but there is no mending it now. You can never, never, come back."

Tanial straightened up and glared at Molsemis. "No mistake! My spirit has been among you like a swan with a broken wing. When I hear my own language spoken, then the wing will heal, and my spirit will fly."

Molsemis sighed. "I will help you," he said.

9) The Star Trail

He telleth the number of the stars;
he calleth them all by their names.
                    —PSALM 147:4

Southward across the black sky tramped the star bear. The two hunters trailed him eternally with their star pot. Near the bear danced seven star children. In a hungry time, their parents would give them no food for a children's feast. The children held their dance, however. And, being small, and light with hunger, they danced themselves gently up into the sky.

Tanial shivered under Talaz's blanket. He pressed against Molsemis' warm back. Loud as a musket shot, a tree cracked in the cold. Another seemed to answer down by the lake.

Tanial counted the dim star children. He could see all seven. Awasos had been proud of that, as he had been proud of all Tanial's skills.

Tanial's sleepy gaze drifted across the sky to the star road. Awasos had said that this long shimmer of stars was the path of the dead. "Jamie's on that road," Tanial thought. "Mhlosses said—wait a minute."

Tanial sat up abruptly. He shivered from both cold and tension. His movement pulled the blanket off Molsemis, who rolled over and groaned. "What is it, Tanial?"

"Molsemis!" Tanial was ashamed to find his teeth chattering. "We left no tracks for Azo and Sozap, did we?"

"No tracks."

"But what about Mhlosses?"

"Mhlosses is asleep in his warm wigwam."

"Molsemis, think about this. Mhlosses speaks with spirits. Spirits told him where to find the moose. You remember?"

"I remember."

"Maybe spirits will tell him where to find *me*."

"Maybe. But he will not send anyone after you."

"Why not?"

"You are not that important, Tanial. They would like revenge, but not that much. They will not face Real Adders to catch you."

At these words, Tanial learned that he could be too cold to shiver. "This river . . . with the beaver house . . . is it in Adder Country?"

"No, but snakes do not lie always in their holes. Lie down, brother—and give me half the blanket."

Numbly Tanial lay down. Trees cracked like shots in the forest. *"Ko-ko-khas, ko-ko-khas!"* called an owl, claiming his hunting grounds. Far away another challenged, *"Ko-ko-khas!"*

"You knew this," Molsemis reminded Tanial. "When you tied the skates on your feet, you knew the Real Adders might be about."

Mournfully Tanial admitted, "That is true."

"Once you reach Beaver River you will be safe from Azo and Sozap. Mhlosses may still come after you in some other way."

"What other way?"

59

"He may slink along your trail in the shape of a wolf."
Molsemis spoke seriously, but Tanial chuckled. "Is that
all he can do?"

"He may send spirits hunting you."

"I think I can handle spirits!"

Molsemis was annoyed. "Ho, brother, handle them then!
Ask me no more questions." He wriggled and resettled himself. Tanial felt cold air at his back.

More humbly, he explained, "I would rather face evil
spirits than Real Adders. That is all I meant."

Molsemis humped himself farther under the blanket.
With angry relish, he remarked, "First, you face Azo and
Sozap!"

"But we have left them far behind!"

"For now."

Tanial had not believed his courage could sink so low.
"Will they find us without a trail?"

"Maybe. If they are that angry. Now sleep, Tanial, and let
me sleep. We leave here when the moon sets."

A full moon was sliding between the branches of a giant
oak. Clearly drawn on its face, an old woman stirred boiling
corn in her pot. She laughed down at Tanial, cold and hungry in the snow. He drew a bit of moose meat from his
pouch and chewed it. "Molsemis," he whispered, "are you
hungry?" But Molsemis was breathing deeply, suddenly
asleep.

Tanial pushed closer to his warmth. The laughing old
woman in the moon made him feel lonely. After Beaver
River he would be really alone with the bear, the hungry
dancing star children, and the spirit road.

But there was another way of looking at the stars. There
was a song Father used to sing, tramping home from Evening Service in Penacook. (Those endless services were an
unpleasantness Tanial remembered from the world of the

giant Yengi. They were different from Mhlosses' spirit conferences and not nearly as interesting. He remembered an agony of boredom, deadly cold, and the ache of restrained muscles.) Very softly, Tanial sang what he remembered:

> "Ye starry lights, ye twinkling flames,
> Shine to your Maker's praise,
> Shine to your Maker's praise.
> He built those worlds above
> And fixed their wondrous frame,
> By His command they stand or move,
> And ever speak His name,
> And ever speak His name. . . ."

The barely remembered song calmed Tanial's thumping heart; he felt himself sinking. As the song trailed into silence, Tanial sank into the black sky, and found himself standing on the spirit road.

Dead Jamie came wandering toward him over the twinkling mist. He still wore his nightshirt—and his bright soft hair. Stumbling aimlessly, he looked around with sleepy blue eyes. He did not see Tanial.

A tall figure came striding up the stars. Hawk feathers stood in his hair. Quill embroidery flashed on his moccasins.

(Tanial remembered those moccasins running toward him, standing at his head. Their quills gleamed in the light of his burning home.

Natanis had just pushed dead Jamie out of the way and raised his tomahawk again. Awasos ran up and caught his arm.

Breath and fear together returned to Daniel. He did not understand the brothers' words, he could only watch them argue. For a long moment they stomped around him, Natanis swinging the tomahawk, Awasos restraining him. Tanial knew now what Awasos had said: "The boy is strong, good-looking. He can keep up with us. I want him! Look, I'll give you the beaver quiver you always liked."

At that time Awasos had considered Daniel as a valuable, possession, not to be wasted. But soon afterward, he began to consider him as a person, someone to like, someone to teach. He found that Daniel could be lifted out of his weak selfish Yengi heritage. Daniel could become Tanial, a real person, and Awasos' son.)

Now Jamie looked up fearlessly at the approaching Indian. "Uncle Awasos," he said in his high, very young voice, "have you seen my brother Dan?"

Awasos bent and took Jamie's hand. He led him past Tanial, saying "Come with me, nephew. Do not wait here for Tanial Waligit. He will be a long time coming."

Tanial woke, freezing. Molsemis had yanked off the blanket and was putting on his snowshoes. He said shortly, "The moon is gone. We go."

As the morning whitened, Molsemis led Tanial steadily uphill and inland. Tanial noticed him pausing on the ridge tops to look down their back trail.

"Molsemis," he asked once, "what will you do if they catch us?"

Molsemis shrugged. "Maybe talk. Like mouse to fox." He pushed off again, crunching along on creaking snowshoes. Stepping in Molsemis' tracks, Tanial barely kept up. In places, the snow reached his knees.

The morning brightened. Gray birch shone green and orange; gray shadows deepened to blue. When the sun was high and the snow sparkle hurt Tanial's eyes, Molsemis stopped. He pointed downhill. "Beaver River."

Tanial squinted down across thicket and windfall. A long gleam of ice wound along a valley. Its banks were fringed with willows and frozen cattails. Before it vanished southward it widened into a silver pool of ice.

The beaver house was a mass of sticks near the entrance of the pool. But the house was broken. Its top was ripped off. Its sticks and branches lay scattered about the ice.

Lean, strong figures moved around the broken beaver house.

Tanial caught his breath. Molsemis grabbed his arm and hauled him down. Together they fell flat on the crust.

10) Real Adders

I make death, singing!
I hack bones, singing!
I make death, singing!
—MICMAC SONG

Tanial pressed his nose to the snow. The sun was almost warm on his back; his stomach froze. He dared not wriggle, or lift a hand.

After a long time Molsemis hissed in his ear, "Thicket." Lifting his nose cautiously from the snow, Tanial saw an alder thicket slightly downhill. Molsemis' dark profile was turned toward that thicket. Hope gleamed in his sidelong glance.

They would certainly be safer, hidden in the thicket. But how to reach it? Molsemis muttered, "Watch Adders north of beaver house. When they are not looking, touch me. I watch Adders south. I touch you. When both touch—move!"

Tanial marvelled at Molsemis' cool observation. He was right—the Adders were divided into two groups. Tanial had not dared to look at them before. Now he watched his group on the north with cautious interest. It was like watching wolves from hiding.

There were five Adders in his group. They ranged around the near shore of the pond, hauling brush onto the ice. Their deerskins were much fringed and beaded. They walked in a grand, proud style, as though they owned the ice and the shining hills beyond. Tanial had to remind himself that they were only mortal men, tiny in the immense wilderness, and isolated in enemy country.

Three of the men had long black scalp locks swinging from their belts. One had a second scalp dangling from his quiver. As he turned toward Tanial, half of his face shone sticky red. But the face looking uphill showed no pain or tension. The redness was not blood but paint. The man was painted for war. His keen eyes ringed with white were checking the hillside.

Just before the Adder's gaze met his, Tanial shut his eyes. He and Molsemis in their gray, tattered deerskins might be taken for stumps, fallen branches, or shadows. But the answering gaze of a human eye, even at that distance, would betray them.

A chickadee called in the woods. The sun warmed Tanial's back. After a while, he squinted.

Two Scalps had turned away.

Molsemis' fingers touched Tanial's wrist. All his Adders must be looking the other way, but two of Tanial's Adders were looking uphill. When they looked away, Two Scalps was turning back to the hillside. Again Tanial felt the pressure of Moslemis' fingers. Again he could not respond.

One of the Adders bent over a brush pile. Two Scalps strode off across the pond to speak to one of Molsemis' Adders. The other three were hacking brush from the beaver house.

Tanial grabbed Molsemis' fingers; Molsemis grabbed back. With a running, swimming motion, they flung themselves downhill behind the alders.

Tanial would have dived right into the alders, but Molsemis held him back. The noise of breaking twigs would surely carry to the pond. Face to snow, behind the alder screen, Tanial waited to hear a shout from the pond. Then would come a crunching rush. The horde of fleet, powerful, well-armed man hunters would run them down before they could even gain the hilltop. But he heard only soft voices and the whack of an ax on ice.

Slowly he looked up from the snow. Under his nose he saw a pair of clasped hands. He and Molsemis had never let go of each other's hands!

And Tanial still did not let go. He looked past their hands, through the alder screen, and saw Two Scalps returning. Over the Real Adder's half-red face, his black scalp lock stood up like a thick mane. Tanial had heard tell of the Adders' scalp lock. It served as a challenge, defiance and trophy to a hostile world. The stiff brush of black hair crowning the bald head was indeed a ferocious, startling sight. A gray feather, fastened across the mane, flashed in the noonday sun.

The quiver thumped on Two Scalps' shoulder as he strode. The long scalp dangling from it swung free. It, too, was red-smeared. But this red was not paint; this was fresh blood.

Tanial shrank inside, remembering his dream. He knew with sudden certainty whose scalp decorated that quiver. Molsemis' hand clenched in his. Molsemis knew it, too.

Tanial stole a glance at Molsemis' face and saw the nostrils squeezed, the forehead tight. No sound escaped. Slowly, the fist in Tanial's hand relaxed. Molsemis breathed again, and so did Tanial.

Now the Adders were chopping holes all over the pond. Tanial's fear-frozen mind began to see what they were doing. Having routed out and eaten the beavers, they were now going to fish through the ice. When they had eaten everything in the pond, they would go back to man-hunting. For that was what Two Scalps' paint said. They were hunting Abenakis, for fun and glory.

Meanwhile they talked and laughed among themselves, exactly like ordinary human beings.

A jay called. Behind Tanial, snowshoes creaked.

Tanial imagined Sozap humping over the horizon in full view of the alerted Adders. He almost hissed a warning.

The creaking came over the hilltop and continued steadily downhill. It passed a short way south of the alder thicket. It was not Azo or Sozap, for Two Scalps was grinning—a bright grin like Adagi's. He raised a broad hand in salute.

From the corner of his eye, Tanial watched the newcomer glide past. His back was turned to the alders. His scalp lock bristled over a shining bald head. Bear-claw earrings jiggled on his shoulders, a blond scalp floated from his belt, and a fox tail from one knee thong. This proud figure raised a hand to Two Scalps, and crunched on down to the pond.

Dropping their axes, the Adders gathered at the edge of the ice. They closed in around the snowshoer, questioning, listening. He talked in a low but triumphant voice and pointed behind him uphill.

Under cover of the Adder voices, Molsemis whispered, "He scouted the camp!"

Tanial gulped in horror. This Adder scout, crouched in a thicket, had watched old Talaz hopping about, he had watched Nolka bent over her embroidery. Tanial had felt this same horror once before when a dark hand pushed through a broken cabin door. He exclaimed in a strangled whisper, "My sister!" He did not mean Hannah.

Down on the ice, the Adders were whooping and brandishing knives. The scout was gesturing, almost dancing, a description of the camp. There were Talaz's hop and Adagi's strut. And who was the waddler with outthrust chest? The scout shook a brawny fist, and Tanial recognized Katetin. The Adders laughed, their faces shone with confidence. Already they felt the scalps at their belts!

After the happy conference, three of them got onto snowshoes and entered the woods. The boys heard them crunching away, west and southwest.

When the sound of their going had died, Molsemis whispered, "Tonight I go back, warn Azo and Sozap. Hurry to camp."

"We, *we* warn the camp."

"Not you. They see you, they shoot."

This was true. Tanial was forever cut off from Natanis' band. He would never even learn their fate. Loneliness like a cold wave swept over him. He had left the only tribe he had. The Yengis were strangers after all, maybe imaginary strangers. He had not seen a white face in five years. But Katetin he knew; she was a real woman who had been kind to him—sometimes. He thought of her feeding Talaz and of her sparing Nolka's puppy. Adagi's face rose before him, laughing; Nolka held out the little bag to him. By nightfall their scalps might swing beside Awasos' hair.

If Tanial had been alone here with this terrible knowledge, he would have had to go back. He would have had to brave Natanis' hate and the others' anger, and seize the very slim chance of forgiveness. But God had sent Molsemis after him.

Molsemis whispered, "You skate through Adders."

Tanial thought he could not have heard right. He actually turned his head and looked at Molsemis.

With a stiff, barely moving finger, Molsemis sketched a

68

route. "Sneak to river. Careful not to crunch. Skate very fast like a bird, like a spirit. Gone before they see you."

"What about the dam?" There should be a beaver dam, but it was hidden behind willows.

"Not big. Jump."

Tanial cracked a frozen smile. He almost saw himself doing it! If the Adders were as unfamiliar with skates as the Abenakis, they might take him for a spirit! Certainly there was no safety for him in the snow, between the Adders, the scouts, and Azo and Sozap.

Down on the ice, the Adders returned to their fishing. They had time to catch every fish in the pond before the foolish Abenakis broke camp! That was what the Adders thought.

Two Scalps was closest. He stood over his hole, bobbing his lure, spear poised. A stray wind lifted Awaso's hair from his shoulder. It streamed on the wind.

Sorrow and hate jostled each other in Tanial's heart, but fear lay closest to the surface. On top of fear, he tried to feel brave confidence. Over and over he tried to see himself flying through the Adders. As to what would happen if he stumbled—he shoved that thought down in his mind, along with hate and sorrow.

Slowly the sun faded. Tanial was first aware that his back was as cold as his stomach. Then he noticed that blue shadows were now gray. Long streamers of cloud came drifting over the sky. Father used to call those clouds "mares' tails." New snow would be coming behind them.

Light withdrew from the trees. The ice on the pond turned dull green. The Adders merged with dusk. Finally Tanial and Molsemis could only hear them, talking together.

Molsemis moved. He pulled his stiff hand out of Tanial's, and sat up.

Tanial tried to sit up, but he was frozen where he lay. He

69

worked stiff fingers under, and ripped his shirt away from the snow. Kneeling up, he thought his back was broken. The misery in his stomach was hunger, he hoped, not terror.

On the pond, red light danced. A gathering flame pushed back darkness. Powerful silhouettes stalked around the fire. Now the fire broke into many small fires. Adders were carrying torches here and there over the ice.

Two Scalps brought to his hole a torch that painted half of him with red light. He jammed the torch into the ice and took up his spear. With one side red, the other side night-black, he looked like a condemned man, painted for burning.

The savage thought rose in Tanial's mind, "I wish you were, Two Scalps! I wish you were!" For now he knew clearly that he had loved his "father" Awasos.

Molsemis slipped off his snowshoes so they would not crunch as he stole away, and pushed a small object into Tanial's hand. It was Azo's clay pipe. With it, he gave Tanial a handful of red willow scraps. He whispered, "Give this to the river, so he will carry you safely. Or smoke it, for hunger."

Tanial hauled out of his pouch all the meat his fingers found. It was all he had to give Molsemis.

"For speed back to camp, brother."

Molsemis gulped the meat down. That was the easiest way to carry it. He pressed Tanial's hands and went. A gray shadow, he merged with the night.

Tanial lifted the skates. He looked at Talaz's blanket, left crumpled on the snow. Molsemis had left it for him, but he saw no way to carry it through the gauntlet of torches on the ice. He would have to fly like a bird, entirely free. Very regretfully he left it behind.

Slowly he stepped downhill. Trees were cracking and snapping with cold, and Tanial tried to time his steps to

sound like tree crackings. He hoped, too, that the voice of
the fire would cover his noise. But the hard crust crackled
with every step and every stumble. With each crackle Tanial
froze, and looked down through the trees. Sometimes he
heard voices speaking. Once a loud voice called a question,
and laughter answered from all around the pond. Tanial
waited, frozen in his tracks, until a tree cracked like a musket shot. Then, stepping high like a moose, he ventured another yard downhill.

He bumped into trees. Twigs ran into his eyes. By the time
he reached the river, he felt that half the night was gone.

There was the ice, smooth and black. At the near bend, a
warning reflection of firelight glowed.

Tanial sat down on the bank. In the dark he fitted the
skates on his feet, and bound the thongs up his legs. Putting
on skates was putting on power. In his mind he again saw
himself zooming past and among the Adders, and this time
he believed it! To make extra sure, he drew the flight feather
from his pouch and thrust it into his hair. Feathered for
flight, winged-footed, he glided gently up the black river.

The ice turned blue, shot with white light. Tanial glanced
up at the black branches drifting past. A full, white moon
was looking down. This was not good. Firelight was bad
enough. Firelight with moonlight would be almost like day.

"I will have to go faster," he thought confidently. "At
least I will not stumble, blind." He could see every twig,
every dimple in the ice.

He came to the bend and jerked to a stop.

Before him opened the beaver pond. Directly in front
sprawled the beaver house. Its sticks and branches littered
the ice. Tanial saw that he would have to veer far left, on
clear ice. Out in the middle of the pond the fire bloomed like
a big red flower. There he would swoop right. That way he
would pass close to Two Scalps. But the left side of the pond

was aflame with torches. Most of the Adders were gathered
there.

Tanial pressed one toe against the ice. "My God," he
thought, "make haste to help me." And to be sure he added,
"Oho, ho, ho, make haste to deliver me." Lightly he touched
the feather in his hair, and the Bible in his pouch. Then he
pushed off.

The ice murmured deeply. Tanial whooshed left around
the beaver house and out on the clear, blue pond. The fire
ahead was bigger than he had thought. Sooner than he had
planned, Tanial swooped right.

An Adder yelled. A flung torch flew at Tanial's head. He
doubled down. The flying flame hissed over his shoulder.
Rising on the same stroke, he saw Two Scalps' astonished
face zooming toward him.

Half-red, half-black, Two Scalps stood defiantly over his
fishing hole, his fire-reflecting eyes wide with disbelief. He
thought Tanial was a spirit, a mysterious being of the enemy
forest. Even so, he hefted his spear.

Tanial threw himself into the air and aside.

The leap seemed to last long moments. Tanial had never
in his life seen so clearly. Directly under his skates was a
heap of golden perch. If he had not leaped he would have
hit the heap, and stumbled. Torches sped toward him from
the left. The torches lit angry faces. Or—Tanial almost
laughed—could they be frightened faces?

He sailed past Two Scalps' outflung arm. Two Scalps
looked at Tanial over his muscled shoulder. His eyes were
no longer astonished; they were narrow slits of fury. Two
Scalps had seen that Tanial was only a human being, something that could be killed.

Back on the ice he bent double, jabbed his blades and
pumped. Over the shouts and the hiss of torches, he heard a

crash and skitter close to his left. A tomahawk whirled on the smooth ice.

Tanial went into a long, strong glide. He straightened up—and saw, dead ahead, what had not been obvious from the hillside.

Two long strokes ahead, the pond ended. The river wandered on south, narrow and dark under overhanging trees. But across the mouth of the river, between pond and river, stretched the beaver dam. And it was huge.

11) The Ice Trail

Saith the spirit,
"Dream, oh, dream again,
And tell of me.
Dream, thou."
—WINNEBAGO SONG

Molsemis had remembered wrong. "Not big," he had said. "Jump." But the beaver dam was taller than Tanial. It was an old dam, mended and rebuilt over many years. Great drifted trunks were caught in it, branching birches, willow saplings. Tanial was zooming toward it too fast for thought. Behind him the ice thudded and shook under running feet. There was no time to make for the bank and scramble around. He would have to fly over the dam, like the spirit he pretended to be.

He shoved off the other foot. The dam rushed up to him. A trunk stuck out near the bottom of the dam. Moonlight glanced off its rough tip. Tanial leaped for it. He lifted himself into the air, tapped the trunk with a skate blade, and soared higher. Stick tangles and night-black holes gaped for his feet.

With his hands he caught the topmost branches. Before him he saw the river winding south, dark and quiet.

74

He flung his feet out and landed on top, on his knees. He slid on his stomach across a mass of frozen sticks. Kicking his feet over the dam, he hung for a second, looking back. Snarling, Two Scalps swarmed up the dam. A knife gleamed in his fist. Close behind, the pack came pounding. Tanial pushed himself off backward, and dropped to the river ice.

He whirled and pumped. Black ice zipped by, close under his nose. Bars of moonlight whizzed between bars of shadow.

Tanial screeched around three bends, while behind him the Adders' screams faded. He slowed, and glanced over his shoulder.

Moonlit ice stretched clear behind him. The river rumbled gently under his skates. There came no thudding echo of following feet.

Tanial remembered Molsemis' confident whisper, "You skate through Adders." That was what he had done! Had Molsemis watched from the hilltop? Tanial hoped so, and grinned. Then he shook the foolish thought away. By now, Molsemis should be well along the trail back to camp. At this moment, he should be warning Azo and Sozap.

It would be well, Tanial realized, to put a deal of ice between himself and the Adders, for they were tireless hunters. Falling into an easy rhythm of long, slow strokes, he wandered with the river into blacker night.

Safe for the moment, Tanial began to feel his hurts. His knees complained. They had slammed down hard on the rough beaver dam. Held tight in stiff lacings, his feet were frozen. His stomach was a mass of cuts and bruises and punctures from the dam. Worst of all, his legs were tiring. The skates had no middle section, under the arch. "I should have on Yengi boots, not moccasins."

When the ache in calf and arch became unbearable, Tanial glided to the bank and sat down. He unlaced the skates and stood them on their blades in the snow. Rubbing his tingling feet, he looked around.

The moon was setting. Long bars of level moonlight still reached between black trees, but the sky was graying. Tanial shivered. Active, he had been unaware of the intense cold. Now his teeth chattered. The cold was as much inside him as outside.

The gray sky turned white. Tanial thought of eating a bit of moose, but his hand would not grasp the pouch. He looked down at the hand and saw it clenched in a tight fist. How long had his hands been clenched?

"Very well," he told his hands, "rest." He leaned back against an overhanging root. The whitening world blurred, and dimmed.

Night seemed to return. Slowly a red glow warmed the air. The glow came from a tame fire burning in a stone fireplace. A slim figure stood between Tanial and the fire. Firelight reddened the side of her gray homespun dress. Sunny hair spilled from under her kerchief. Her back turned to Tanial, she was looking down at something in her hands.

Tanial murmured, "Hannah."

"Hannah turned around. He smelled the warm fragrance of the loaf she held. "Dan!" She leaned toward him, her blue eyes urgent. "Dan, don't sleep. What are you doing sleeping? Hurry. Pray and skate. Don't sleep." Firelight flickered down her gray skirt and faded, and Hannah, fire, and hearth sank into the darkness behind Tanial's closed eyes.

He came awake knowing what he had tried not to know for five years. "Hannah is dead," he told himself. He tried thinking it again. "Hannah is dead because she tried to save Jamie and me."

76

Even if he skated the length of the river, even if he found a settlement of dark, close houses and loud Yengis, he would never find Hannah. She was with Jamie and Awasos on the star-trail.

Saying it did not make it more true than before, but when Tanial opened his eyes, he seemed to see more clearly. "And it's not true that the Yengis are evil," he said aloud. "They are only people like the Abenakis, maybe even like the Adders." Among themselves, even the Adders seemed like human people! "And the Yengis are *my* people."

Sunlight dazzled on the ice, but over the sky spread a film of milky clouds. "Those mares' tails yesterday were a true sign," Tanial thought. "Snow is coming." Flexing his frozen hands, he made them grasp the skates and lace them on his rested feet.

Before setting out, he felt in his pouch and Nolka's bag for meat. His hand passed over the Bible and came to something hard and stringy. Meat? He pulled it out. It was Molsemis' gift of red willow. He heard again Molsemis' whisper, "Give this to the river so he will carry you safely." And Hannah had said "Pray."

"Good idea." Tanial pushed himself stiffly up, and away from the bank. From northern bend to southern bend, the river was silent, empty. The Adders must have given up the chase.

Tanial glided out to the middle. There he stopped, held up his hands full of bark, and called "Oho!"

A flutter of chickadees answered from the bank bushes.

"Oho, ho, ho!" Tanial prayed aloud, "Listen, Father River! I give you this good smoking willow. I would build a fire here and burn it for you, but I must make speed." He paused and scattered a pinch of bark on the ice.

"Oho, Father River! Snow comes to cover you. When the snow falls, I must be far south. Father River, carry me there." He scattered most of the bark.

"Oho, ho, ho! Hold me up, Father River! Do not crack or melt before me. Do not lay twigs before my skates."

Tanial looked at the last pinch of willow. "Or smoke it for hunger," Molsemis had said. Hunger growled in Tanial's stomach, and he was short of meat. He glanced up, and saw cold, milky clouds spreading fast over the sky.

"Oho, ho, Father River! I give you all my willow! Give me a safe road south." Tanial tossed the last of the bark on the ice, and pushed off.

Close under the banks, rocks broke through the ice. Fallen branches littered the river edges. But Tanial kept to the middle, where the ice was clear, hard, and blue.

Skating with long, free strokes, he dug into his pouch for meat. Finding none, he turned Nolka's little bag inside out. It was empty. He had not counted on sharing with Molsemis!

"You can go three times farther on moose meat than on any other meat," he told himself. His stomach growled denial.

Tanial stuffed the little bag into his pouch and skated on, watching the bare branches drift overhead. He might, by some small chance, see a porcupine clinging there. He could kill it with a stone. And then he could save the quills for Nolka to press and dye, and work into embroidery.

Tanial jerked himself out of this daydream. He would not be seeing Nolka again. Nolka might even be dead now, as Awasos was dead, and Hannah and Jamie were dead, and Father also might well be dead. Cut off from both his worlds, alone in winter silence, Tanial swung stubbornly over the ice.

The ice rumble beneath him was the only sound. At every bend he paused, looking for Adders or for a rough, permanent cabin. But the forest glided endlessly by, empty,

78

dreamlike. Snow clouds covered the sun. All shine and sparkle had died, even from the ice.

Tanial judged it was noon when he had to stop. His moccasined arches screamed for support. He broke tough slabs of rock-maple bark and jammed them into the skates between toe and heel. This gave enough support so that he could skate on till the early winter evening.

In deepening dusk, Tanial swooped to the bank and sank down on a fallen trunk. Panting and trembling, he unlaced the skates. Desperately he scrabbled in his pouch for one stray scrap of meat. He found nothing but the Bible.

"That Bible is one heavy thing," he thought dreamily. He lifted it out and laid it on the snow. "I will skate faster without it."

A light wind turned the Bible's yellow pages. Just so, Father used to ruffle through, hunting a passage to read to Hannah and Dan. Tanial remembered him best like that, hunched over the Bible, firelight soft on his rugged face.

Far back in the forest a voice called. The cry was long-drawn, high and thin. Could it be wind?

The Bible pages fluttered down and lay flat. For the moment the wind had died. But the voice called again.

Tanial grabbed the Bible. Heavy or not, he needed its magic. For he recognized the voice in the forest.

He had heard it often from the safety of Awasos' wigwam. He had heard it, too, from the lesser safety of a campfire. But now he was hearing it from a place of no safety at all. He was alone in the darkening forest, too exhausted to rise and skate away.

And the voice that rose and fell, nearer every moment, was the voice of a wolf pack.

12) Hunted

Mountains tremble at my yell!
I strike for life!

—OJIBWA SONG

Awasos gave little thought to wolves. "Wolves will not brave
you," he had told Tanial, "unless . . ." What was the "unless"? And had Awasos ever huddled behind a fallen tree,
unarmed, while a pack swept toward him?

Tanial slid down behind the trunk. The pack was silent
now; he could not guess how close it was.

The dark woods were quiet, but for a rising wind. Tanial
was glad to feel the wind on his face. It was coming from the
wolves to him. At least they would not get scent of him.

Snow crunched; two crunches, pause, two crunches. Tanial heard harsh, panting breath.

What would leap and pause? What would break the crust
with each leap? "It's a little jumping deer," he decided.
Straining his eyes, he caught its motion. A noisy shadow, it
was bounding slowly toward him through underbrush.

Seeing the ice, it paused. Tanial watched its long neck
shoot up and down. Turning its head, it looked around for

80

another path to safety.

The pack broke silence, right behind the deer.

Tanial jumped. Then he shrank down as low as he could behind the trunk, worming his way into the snow.

He heard more crunches, and a hollow rumbling of ice. The deer had floundered onto the river.

Panting bodies streamed past Tanial. One passed so close it must have leaped the trunk. Quick shadows darted across darkness and scuffled on the ice. Tanial heard snarls and ripping sounds. The ice continued to rumble.

When Tanial dared turn his head to look, the wolf pack was eating. He counted five long, lean shadows humped over the lump of carcass. Smaller ones trotted about, circling it. One darted in toward it. A big wolf growled. The cub hesitated. Then it turned away, and joined the trotting circle.

The five large wolves tore, gulped, and coughed. Trotting close, two cubs jumped in and grabbed a section of carcass. Snarling, a large wolf stood on the carcass, holding it down. The cubs ripped their section free and dragged it away.

Tanial curled up tight against the rough trunk. His hands and feet were numb. He trembled more from tension than cold. The cold had ebbed somewhat. As he realized this, a soft cold fuzz drifted across his cheek.

Snow was falling.

Now Tanial despaired. Closing his eyes, he relaxed in his freezing bed and gave himself up to hunger. The sound of chawing and chomping so close by was a torture. "One thing I will do," he thought. "I will eat what the wolves leave. I can die on a full stomach."

Sometime later he opened his eyes on total darkness. Had the wolves gone? Listening, Tanial made out breathing, padding sounds. He strained his eyes into the darkness, and saw light.

Lightning hovered over the river.

81

Tanial blinked, and brushed soft snow from his eyelids. He knew that hunger could help one see spirits.

He was hungry enough, and tired enough—and here came a spirit. The steady lightning hovered, glowing. As he watched, it bounced playfully upward. Red light flashed into lines, sketched on the black air. High above the ice a face took shape. It was an ancient, crumpled face. Forehead and sunken cheeks were bright lightning wrinkles. The nose hooked like a grasping hand.

Tanial gaped.

Blue lightning drew whizzing whirlpools of eyes. The red lips grinned, blue fangs shone through.

If Tanial could have breathed, he would have cried out.

Now the ghastly face bounced about, flapping wings of long red hair. In its soft glow, Tanial saw two young wolves playing together. They bounded and rolled on the ice like puppies, paying no attention to the Great Head.

The Head flew zigzag back and forth along the river. Terrified, Tanial realized that it was hunting him.

And then he remembered Molsemis' warning. "Mhlosses may still come after you ... He may send spirits hunting you." And Tanial had answered, "I would rather face evil spirits than Real Adders."

And he had faced Real Adders!

Tanial laughed aloud. His laughter broke through the hiss of falling snow, and through the mists in his mind. The Great Head had wandered upriver. Now it turned and sped back to him. In its returning light he saw the young wolves reared together, forepaw to forepaw, looking toward him.

He jumped to his feet. He shook off the gathered snow and yelled at the Head, "Oho, Mhlosses! Is that the best you can do?"

13) The Stranger

I am become a stranger unto my brethren;
and an alien unto my mother's children.
                                        —PSALM 69:8

The Head swooped toward him. Blue fangs chattered.
Whirling eyes flashed blue fire.

Tanial roared laughter at it. He shouted, "Mhlosses, you
send me good news! By this I know that you and my friends
are alive!"

The Head paused. Its eyes stretched out long, the mouth
turned down. The blue lips trembled, as though about to
cry. Its only power lay in Tanial's fear. It only existed in his
eyes.

Beginning with the flapping wings of hair, the Head
faded. The eyes faded last, and the red glow went out like a
snuffed candle. Tanial stood triumphant, alone in total
darkness.

He was beyond fear. "I am Tanial Waligit," he sang. "I
flew among Adders. I am Daniel Abbott!" Singing, he
hopped in a close-circled dance. If only he could keep warm
and awake till morning, he would find food out on the ice.

Air currents whirled. Tanial heard the pad of paws nearby. "I am Tanial Waligit who killed the moose," he shouted to the wolves. "I am Daniel Abbott who conquered the Great Head!" The louder he sang, the braver he felt. Unhungry, the wolves were not likely to attack—certainly not while he danced and roared! They did not know he could not see in the dark! If only he had a little drum now like Mhlosses' tom-tom, this would be a real celebration. Lacking a drum, he clapped the rhythm.

Dancing, Tanial lifted himself, soaring, out of despair. But when black night began to lift, he was near exhaustion.

He sank down on the fallen trunk and felt around for the skates. They were buried in soft, new snow. Daylight was gray when he found them. Glancing around, he saw that the ice had vanished.

The river was soft and white, fluffed with a foot of snow.

Thoughtfully, Tanial rubbed his aching legs. "Couldn't have skated anyhow," he tried to comfort himself. "Legs are skated out."

He worked the frozen laces out of the skates and stuffed them into Nolka's bag. He left the skates in the snow, and staggered down to the river.

Out in the middle lay a snow-fuzzed mound; the remains of the wolf feast. Tanial stumbled out to it. Crouching, he brushed off the snow.

Bloody pieces of a young buck littered the ice. The carcass was so mangled and torn that Tanial could easily rip off bits with his hands.

At first he tore off small bits and gulped them down. When his stomach accepted these, he went to work on a bigger piece to carry with him. Gradually he began to notice a tingling at the back of his neck. He had been tingling for some time, but hunger had taken all his attention.

He yanked off a hunk of meat, dropped it in the pouch,

and looked over his shoulder.

A large wolf watched him from the bank. The gray of its coat merged with the gray of the woods. Falling snow speckled and blurred its outline. Tanial might not have seen it at all except for the yellow glow of its eyes.

He rose and stepped around the carcass, so as to face the wolf. He grinned at it, and went back to ripping meat.

Grayness moved in the snow mist behind the wolf. Another pair of yellow eyes watched Tanial.

He tore off a last shred and stood up, chewing. With food, his courage swelled. He called cheerfully to the big wolf, "Ho, Molsem, Wolf Brother, I leave you the rest! Look, I take only one thing more."

A black hoof had caught his eye, sticking up out of the snow at a strange angle. Tanial took hold and pulled, and the hoof came free. He held it up for Molsem to see.

"I take this for speed," he explained. "I have great need of speed. All this"—he gestured at the scattered carcass—"is yours."

Tanial turned his back on Molsem and trudged away south. As he stomped along, kicking up clouds of snow, he tied the hoof by a skate thong to his belt. The hoof swung back and forth, hitting his knees and dripping blood on his leggings. He muttered, "God will give me feet like deer's feet." Somewhere in its magic pages, the Bible said something like that.

Tanial's neck tingled again. He swung around, and glimpsed a gray motion at the last bend of the river. Molsem had darted into the woods.

Tanial tried to think. He swayed on his feet. His legs ached naggingly. His brain was fogging fast. He was no longer sure why he was walking on this river. Only the hoof swinging at his belt told him to keep walking. He was looking for something; he knew that much. Now, why was Molsem looking for *him?*

Tanial shrugged and mumbled. He turned south and staggered on. Out of his dimming brain the thought rose, "It's Molsemis! He's following to see if I get there!" Where? He looked over his shoulder, and was glad to see the wolf not far behind. It was trotting in Tanial's footsteps. When Tanial stopped, it stopped. They looked at each other through the steady snowfall.

"Brother," said Tanial. He held out a friendly hand. Molsem cocked his head, his ears pointed forward. He watched Tanial with narrow, golden eyes.

"Hungry?" Tanial remembered now that he had stolen Molsem's meat. "Take this, brother." He drew a hunk of meat from his pouch, and tossed it to Molsem.

"Eat that, and come," he told the wolf. "Come see what I, Tanial Waligit, will do." He was going to do something. Later he would remember what. He grinned at Molsem, who stood quietly over the meat, watching.

Tanial raised a hand in salute and turned south. He struggled on, the reminding hoof whacking his knees at every step.

He sank down, and found himself sprawled in the snow. "Molsem!" He called. He rolled over and looked around. Only blowing whiteness met his dreamy gaze.

But something drifted on the wind. Tanial sniffed, and sniffed again, and drew in a fair whiff of the good smell. His stomach rose and turned over.

He called, "Hannah!"

He floundered to his feet, and headed into the smell.

The smell led Tanial up the bank and into the woods. Crashing through undergrowth, he stumbled onto a trail. The narrow trail curved among gray oaks. Beyond was a clearing. Black oak stumps jutted out of the snow. Across the clearing, smoke rose into the snowfall.

Tanial reeled across the clearing, among the blackened, dead stumps. He fell over buried stumps, and over his feet. Under the smoke was a chimney. Under the chimney a roof sloped, a patch of pure white against the gray-speckled woods. The cabin rose out of the snow to greet him.

It was gray and permanent as a granite boulder. At sight of its rough walls, Tanial's frozen heart melted. Voices and images flooded up from memory.

This was a country of giants. This was a country of permanence, of cleared lands, solid houses, rich oven smells. Feeling like a lone flying swan who sees beneath him his long-lost flock, Tanial shouted "Father! Hannah!"

The door cracked open. Dim against the inside darkness, a stocky figure leaned out.

The overpowering smell from the open door was warm with sweet promise. It was the smell of baking bread. Strangely, the plump girl peering out at Tanial was not Hannah. Her hair was black as Nolka's. Nor was she a giantess; for all her soft bulk, she was shorter than Tanial! But she was Yengi. Her face was white as a snow patch in the dark doorway.

In a burst of clarity, Tanial realized how he must look to her. He saw himself kneeling in the snow, snow-crusted. He saw the swan feather in his hair, the bloody hoof dangling. He remembered Mhlosses' grumblings about the Yengi religion. They had no understanding of magic.

The girl's face whitened even more. She began to close the door.

"No," Tanial called. "No, no!" It was one Yengi word he was sure of. The girl hesitated.

Tanial threw his head back, drew a deep breath, and sang:

"The Lord my shepherd is;
I shall be well supplied;

87

Since He is mine and I am His
What can I want beside?"

The girl leaned farther out. The wind whipped her white
apron around the edge of the door. Tanial sang on:

"He leads me to the place
Where heavenly pasture grows,
Where living waters gently pass
And full salvation flows."

The girl put a hand to her mouth.

Tanial fumbled in his pouch, brought out the Bible, and
held it up for her to see.

She pushed the door wide and came to him in a whirl of
blowing skirts and dark hair. Her strong hands under his
arms hauled him up. Leaning on her shoulder, he staggered
into the cabin.

In here it was as dark as a wigwam and more quiet. Wind
and snow suddenly ceased. Warmth burned Tanial's cheeks.
He felt amazingly sheltered, almost trapped.

The girl helped him to the fireplace. She pulled a bench
forward. Then she went away, and the cabin darkened even
more. Dimly Tanial understood that she had shut the door.

The bench was to sit on. Tanial knew that, but he had
lived for years in wigwams. He lowered himself to the firm
plank floor, and leaned against the bench.

He was looking into a narrow stone fireplace. A tame,
golden fire burned there. A kettle hung on an iron arm, a
baker's shovel leaned beside the fireplace. The smell of new
bread was heavy on the warm air.

A shadow moved between Tanial and the fire. The girl
leaned over him. Firelight reddened the side of her gray
homespun dress. Rough black hair spilled bountifully from

under her kerchief.

"Oh," she said, and shyly touched his hair. When he did not move, she lifted a braid and held it to the light. Golden firelight shimmered on the golden braid.

Tanial smiled relief. Why had he not thought, out there in the snow, to point out his Yengi hair?

She knelt beside him and gently drew the frozen, tattered mocassins from his feet.

Tanial reached up and pulled the flight feather out of his hair. He laid it in his pouch, and after a moment he untied the pouch from his belt and set it away behind him. With numb fingers he untied the deer's hoof and let it fall from him. Magicless, he was no more than himself. He looked up into the girl's face. She hovered over him, helpful and curious.

The Yengis were known to be indifferent, even cruel to one another, but this girl was friendly. When her rough, loud-voiced menfolk came home, she would speak to them, and they would accept him. One day she might be Daniel's friend, maybe close like a sister.

With a pang like homesickness, he remembered his real sister. He seemed almost to glimpse her, shadowy in the tame firelight. Her round, dark face smiled at him; she stretched out a hand to him. From her scarred and stubby fingers dangled the half-embroidered bag.

A warm flame hissed and stretched upward, dispelling shadow. The vision faded.

Daniel untied the little bag from his belt, only to loop it around his neck. It dropped down inside his shirt and swung against his chest, where his heart was thumping slower, calmer, almost gently.

Postscript

According to legend, Abenaki Indians captured young Daniel Abbott during a raid on Penacook (now Concord), New Hampshire, and carried him off to the Lake Champlain area. A strong and active fellow, Daniel did well with the Abenakis, who were going to adopt him. But Daniel—unlike some white captives who came to prefer Indian life to their own—wanted only to escape.

The Indians were adept on snowshoes but knew nothing of ice skates. By great good luck, Daniel got his hands on a pair of skates, tricked his captors into thinking them useless, put them on, and escaped. After a long, cold, and lonely journey, he arrived home in Penacook. There he subsequently married and raised sixteen children or perhaps he raised eighteen children; on this point, the legend is vague.